Carlo Gébler was born in Dublin in 1954. He lives outside Enniskillen, Co. Fermanagh, Northern Ireland.

He is the author of several novels, including *A Good Day for A Dog* and *The Dead Eight* (shortlisted for the Kerry Group Irish Fiction Award), the short story collection *W9 & Other Lives*, works of non-fiction including the narrative history, *The Siege of Derry* and the memoir *The Projectionist: The Story of Ernest Gébler*. He has also written novels for children as well as plays for radio and the stage, including *10 Rounds*, which was shortlisted for the Ewart-Biggs Prize. He is a member of Aosdána. From 1991 to 1997, he taught creative writing in HMP Maze and from 1997 to 2015 he was writer-in-residence in HMP Maghaberry. He currently works in the community with prisoners who are nearing the end of their sentences.

Also by Carlo Gébler

The Wing
Orderly's Tales

Carlo Gébler

NEW ISLAND

THE WING ORDERLY'S TALES
First published in 2016 by
New Island Books
16 Priory Office Park
Stillorgan
County Dublin
Republic of Ireland

www.newisland.ie

New Island is a member of Publishing Ireland, the Irish book publishers'
association.

PRINT ISBN: 978-1-84840-494-6
EPUB ISBN: 978-1-84840-496-0
MOBI ISBN: 978-1-84840-495-3

British Library Cataloguing Data.
A CIP catalogue record for this book is available from the British Library.

Typeset by JVR Creative India
Cover design by Mariel Deegan
Printed by ScandBook AB, Sweden

LOTTERY FUNDED

Supported by the Arts Council of Northern Ireland.

10 9 8 7 6 5 4 3 2 1

For Euan

'. . . shew thy pity on all captives and prisoners.'

— The Book of Common Prayer

'Everything's got a moral, if you can only find it.'

— Alice in Wonderland, Lewis Carroll

Contents

Author's Note

A wing is a separate section of a building, usually in a jail, and an orderly in such a setting is a prisoner with responsibility for keeping the area clean and tidy.

In the UK penal system (of which Northern Ireland is a part), prisoners currently receive a tiny weekly stipend in return for such duties. They can use their earnings to buy toiletries, tobacco, food and other items from the prison Tuck Shop.

Besides money, the work affords orderlies privileged contact with staff. In the closed, authoritarian and often capricious world of prison, the value of such contact usually outweighs any antagonism orderlies may encounter from other prisoners who disapprove of their close contact with staff.

Prison culture is the foundation of these stories but readers need to remember that this is fiction. The reader may find Belfast on a map but will look in vain for HMP Loanend and YOC Culcavy (which feature in these pages) because they're invented, as are all the characters, none of whom bears any relation to people either living or dead.

The New Boy

Once I was convicted in Belfast Crown Court, I was taken back downstairs and locked in a holding cell. It was cold and manky and on the walls prisoners had scrawled graffiti. It was the usual stuff about fuckwit judges, cruel sentences, paramilitaries, football teams, wives, children, and the scribblers' despair, rage and revenge plans – which mostly involved tearing someone's head off. I'd no tobacco – can you fucking believe it, no smoking in the courthouse – and nothing to read – for some reason no one's ever been able to explain to me, you're not allowed a book in court either – so I stretched out on this bench that was covered in a heavy nasty plastic that smelt of old sweat and spunk and something chemical, and dozed. I didn't want to think.

After a while I heard keys jangling and then the cell door opened and I sat up.

'We're going,' said the Escort screw at the door.

I stood up without thinking and held my arms out, wrists side by side. I knew the drill. That's what jail does: it gets in you and then you do what they want automatically. Like breathing, it just happens.

The Escort cuffed me and brought me out to the yard behind the courthouse and put me in a horsebox. That's what you call a prison van. He stuck me in a wee cubicle about four-foot square with a moulded plastic seat and a high wee window to let light in and tacky patches on the floor. I'd been caught short a few times and had to piss in a horsebox myself so I wasn't surprised.

The cubicle door closed, the key turned. I sat and braced my feet against the wall to push myself back in the seat. I didn't want my new trainers touching the pissy old floor any more than they had to. I heard other cons being loaded on and as they were the horsebox shifted on its axles. Some of them were shouting and swearing. A bad day in court, I guessed.

The engine started and what followed, though I couldn't see out, I knew from all my years in Belfast and all the times I'd gone out to the prison to see mates who were in jail when I was at large. The horsebox trundled out of the courthouse yard and through the city and up the motorway and off the motorway and along several windy little country roads and then finally it reached HMP Loanend. I was let out of the horsebox and taken into the Reception Block and put in a cell and the cuffs were taken off. The grille closed. Another grubby cell with writing on the walls. I sat. I breathed. I waited. There's always waiting in jail. Ninety-nine per cent of the time that's what jail is – waiting around bored out of your fucking mind. The other one per cent is just stupid, vicious bollocks.

After a while an Escort screw arrived, a new one I'd never seen before. He took me over to the wing in the Remand Block where I'd done my time before I went to trial. But I was finished there now. I was convicted, so I would shift to a block for sentenced men.

'Get your stuff,' he said. 'I'll wait.'

I set off down the wing. A prisoner I'd sometimes hung about with on association was coming the other way. He knew I was just back from sentencing and though he'd never ask I knew he was desperate to know my result. I gave him the thumbs down and mumbled a number.

'Oh fuck,' he said.

There was a Day screw floating about who'd been a fixture during my remand time. He unlocked my cell door. I went in. Two Loanend Suitcases sat on my bed, packed and ready because I knew I'd be moving. These are the paper sacks you have to use to lug stuff around. Holdalls and bags are forbidden because the screws reckon you can use them to move contraband. Since you can move gear about in a Loanend Suitcase just as well as in a holdall or a bag, this rule doesn't make any sense. But then the rules in here mostly don't. What they do manage though is to annoy the fuck out of you and to make prison worse. So when it comes to pissing guys off the rules are brilliant.

I grabbed the sacks and left the cell.

'Don't rush back,' said the Day screw who'd unlocked me when I passed him in the corridor a second or two later.

'Thank you for your concern,' I said.

I found the Escort at the circle. He'd retrieved some of my papers from the class office. We went down to the front door and he got more papers from the Door screw who controls all movement in and out of the block from a little room by the door.

'Leaving us then?' shouted the Door screw through the glass that keeps him safe from prisoners.

'Yep.'

'Well, now the fun starts,' he said, smirking. 'We're going to miss you, you know. Send a postcard, won't you? Keep us in the loop.'

'Whatever.'

He went to the touch screen glowing in a dark corner of the room and touched it. The lock clicked and the Escort opened the front door wide. Cold air and grey light flooded in.

'Ladies first,' the Escort screw said.

'Ha, ha,' I said. 'The old jokes are the best.'

I stepped out. A load of starlings were screeching and wheeling overhead and above them there was a lot of cloud the colour of old putty. On remand I'd hopes. But now the hoping was over. I'd just been handed the longest sentence I'd ever got and this was the start of it.

The Escort closed the door behind him. 'That way,' he said. We set off. I led, he followed. We skirted the side of the Remand Block. The grass between the path and the ground floor cells was strewn with empty milk cartons and bits of newspaper and stale bread. Guys who can't be bothered to bin their crap just fuck it out their cell windows. Inside the block itself I could hear shouting and music.

We passed on. Another block with rubbish outside. Then another. Every block the same because in Loanend every block is the same. It's deliberate. They designed it like that to disorientate the cons, and it does. It's also downright depressing, dreary, and monotonous. Everywhere, in every direction, the same buildings with the same walls of grey concrete, the same bars of grey concrete, and the same roofs of grey steel, and in the distance, wherever you look, the same high grey concrete prison perimeter wall topped with razor wire.

We got to Block 3, my new home. The Escort rang the bell and identified himself to the Door screw inside. The door clicked open and we went in and the Escort shouted my details through the glass to the Door screw and we went through the first grille and across the downstairs circle and through another grille and up the back stairs.

'One on,' the Escort screw shouted as we stepped through a wee door at the top and came out onto the circle upstairs. 'F' wing was straight ahead of me and 'E' wing was on my right and to the left was the class office with its huge Perspex windows that allow the screws to observe both wings.

There was a Day screw inside the class office. He saw us and waved. My Escort screw went in. There was my paperwork to do. My arms were aching from the weight of my Loanend Suitcases. I dropped them. I waited. After ten minutes the Escort screw came out.

'Headmaster will see you now,' he said. 'He isn't in the best of form, by the way. Don't say you haven't been warned.'

The Escort screw went across to the little door to the back stairs we'd come through earlier and disappeared. I picked up my Loanend Suitcases and walked over to the class office. The door was open. Like all class office doors, it was in two parts, both opening inwards though in different directions. The bottom half was fixed to the left lintel and was capped with a shelf and the top half was attached to the right lintel and had a handwritten notice stuck to the back with Sellotape: 'The answer is NO! Now what is the question?'

I went in. There was an old desk with the screw behind. The pip on his epaulette identified him as the SO: he was the Senior Officer in charge of 'E' and 'F' wings. He'd thick black hair parted on the left and swept sideways. His face was tanned and his front teeth were crooked, overlapped and very white, like porcelain.

'Chalkman?' he said.

'Yes,' I said.

The room smelt of old foam chair stuffing. Overhead, a fluorescent light hummed. There was a counter under the observation windows. The logbook sat open on top. This is where everything that happens, especially wrongdoings, is recorded. A whiteboard listing the names and prison numbers and cell numbers of the cons on 'E' and 'F' wings hung opposite the counter above a worktop with a Baby Belling stove on it.

I put my Loanend Suitcases down.

'Tired?' he asked. 'I'd offer you a seat but I'm afraid we don't have one.'

There were three greasy easy chairs under the windows but I knew they were for screws and not cons like me.

'Now,' he said, and he looked about his desk. 'Where have you gone? Ah, there we are.' He picked up what he'd found and waved it. 'Your Record Card.'

He began to read what was written on it to himself and as he did his lips moved. I knew what was on there because a few weeks earlier, when the probation officer interviewing me for a pre-sentence report had had to leave the interview room for a moment, I'd fished it out from his folder which he'd left on the desk and read it: it had all my dirt but then that's what the Record Card is for, recording the sort of stuff you'd rather nobody knew:

Chalkman, Harold: prison number 5327X: DOB 18th May 1968: father unknown: put into care by mother at two: married Mavis Chalkman, 1988: two children, Aaron (b. 1986), James (b. 1991): separated from Mavis 2004 while serving 3 years (18 months suspended) for being drunk & disorderly, wrecking house, assaulting wife, etc. Does not take family visits.

5327X is intelligent, manipulative, violent, selfish. His charge sheet and details of time served are attached.

When the SO finished reading he put the card down.

'They call you Chalky don't they?' he said.

I nodded. That was my nickname. Almost everyone in jail has one. Mine wasn't original but at least it was harmless.

'How was court?' he asked.

I didn't answer. I wasn't about to give him the satisfaction.

'Oh dear, he's not speaking. Well, let's see shall we?' He glanced at another sheet of paper with something scribbled on it.

'Twelve years. Crikey!'

I presumed the details were phoned from court. I wasn't surprised. They liked to hear what a con got and the longer the sentence the happier they were.

'Hit a peeler,' he said, 'with a brick during arrest. In the face, wasn't it – Assault Occasioning Actual Bodily Harm? Marvellous. Lucky you didn't get attempted murder. And how many charges of burglary did you ask to be taken in to account?'

I kept my mouth shut.

'Forty-two,' he said, 'which, according to *The Hitchhiker's Guide to the Galaxy*, is also the secret of the universe. That's a novel by the way. Have you heard of it? It's good.'

'I know,' I said, 'I've read it.' This was no sooner out before I wished I hadn't opened my mouth. It annoyed him.

He cleared his throat. He glared. His eyes were abnormally blue. In my experience, megalomaniacs usually have very blue eyes. I was going to have to watch this one. He might be dangerous.

'It's all over with you and the missus, isn't it,' he said, 'because of what you done to her, which wasn't nice, was it? And as a result of your behaviour, you don't take visits, do you?'

My face went red. He saw this and smiled.

'Didn't you hear my question? You don't take visits, do you, because of what you done?'

I couldn't say nothing but I could keep it short. 'No,' I said.

'But, your loss, our opportunity,' he said. 'We need a new orderly for "E" and "F" wings, and, as you don't get visits that means you'll be here, all the time, which is perfect, because that's what the orderly needs to be – here, available, twenty-four seven. So I'm going to volunteer you as our orderly, which will also allow us to keep an eye on you. Obviously you're delighted – brilliant job, great prospects, and orderlies don't have to double up.'

'Aye,' I said, my tone calm, my voice even.

'Yes, Mr Murray,' he said, correcting me.

'Aye, Mr Murray, sir.'

'Sir, is it?'

'Aye, Mr Murray, sir.'

He got up.

'You think you're clever,' he said. 'That makes you stupid. I know I'm stupid. That makes me clever.' I could tell he'd trotted that one out before, many times.

He walked round the desk and stood near me, quite close.

'On "E" and "F" wings,' he said, 'the men are mostly murderers, rapists and armed robbers. They're all doing long sentences and they're all much harder than you'll ever be. So do yourself a favour. Wind your neck in and you just might get out in one piece. Okay?'

I'd heard this kind of spiel before. It was the screws' SOP with a new boy. You scared him and that's how you got him to comply. But as I'd been in jail before, that wasn't going to work with me. Why he hadn't factored that in, I've no idea. Perhaps he just loved acting hard. Perhaps he'd the script so well learnt he'd couldn't go off message. But whatever the case, I wasn't going to show willing. I maintained a blank expression.

'Right,' said Murray. 'Now all we need to do is your TV contract, and then you can move in to your new accommodation.'

He went and sat back down and pushed a piece of paper across the desktop for me to sign, which I did without even reading it. I knew the details already. Every cell in Loanend has a television and you have to sign an agreement for that TV when you move in to your cell. By its terms, you agree to rent the TV for fifty pence a week. That's deducted from your prison wages, which in my case, as an orderly, would be about eight or nine quid a week. You also agree that if your TV gets destroyed you'll keep on paying for it but you won't get a replacement set till you've paid ten quid back to the jail. This clause is supposed to stop riots by making men think, 'Oh no, if I riot my TV will get trashed and I'll have to pay a tenner before I get a new set.' It doesn't stop riots of course but it does stop TVs getting smashed in riots. Now, before they wreck up, cons simply pile their TVs out of harm's way and then kick off.

'You're Cell 11, "F" wing,' said Murray. 'There's a bedding roll and Welcome Pack on the bed. Now fuck off.'

Eskimo

Some months on from the day I arrived. It was morning and I was in bed asleep. I woke when I heard the noise of the key in the lock.

'Morning, Chalky.' The voice was breezy. 'Wakey wakey. Welcome to another day in Wonderland.'

As wing orderly, my unlock time is an hour before the rest of the wing. This is so I can attend to the most important of my duties – cooking the screws' breakfasts. I sat up in bed and watched the steel cell door swing back to reveal Hayes in the corridor beyond. Hayes is one of the nicer Day screws. He is a chunky individual, solid and slow and generally fair.

'What time is it?' I asked.

'If I'd had a quid for every time you asked that question I could retire by now you know,' said Hayes.

I got out of bed. The cell's linoleum floor was cold, a nasty bone-chilling cold. And no wonder. The lino is laid straight onto concrete. I found my flip-flops and got the plastic thingees between my toes.

'And nothing …' Hayes ran a finger and thumb over his lips as he often did. 'Nothing would give me greater pleasure than to get out of this shithole.' He clicked the door into the little keeper that would hold it open through the day.

'You wouldn't retire,' I said.

'Oh yeah?' said Hayes. 'Why's that?'

'Because your life'd be hollow and meaningless without us felons, especially me.'

'You know,' said Hayes, 'I'd never thought about it like that before but now you've put me straight I see you are so fucking right. I just couldn't give you up. Thank you Chalky, you're an inspiration mate.'

The food trolley was beside him. It was painted battleship grey and the paint was chipped. On the top shelf there were several dozen plastic pint milk cartons, the kind with the screw-on green top, all bundled in a plastic cowl. The plastic was slashed. Hayes put his hand through the slash and fished one out.

'Here's your milk, big boy.'

He set the carton on the edge of the wash basin beside my cell door. We get a pint every day. It's the law. A screw once told me they give it out because it's got vitamin D, which stops us going peelywally. Nice theory until you actually look at us. We've all got the prison pallor. The milk doesn't do us any good. The truth, I think, is they give out milk solely because without it we wouldn't be able to drink tea and God help us if we couldn't have our tea. The jail would grind to a halt.

I pulled the curtains. Half the cells in Block 3 face outwards towards the rest of Loanend and the other half face inwards onto the yard around which the block, like every block, is built. My cell then was one of the ones that faced in.

I looked through the concrete bars at the yard with its red gritty floor and its shelter where men huddled to smoke when it rained. It was littered with rubbish left after evening association, or 'asso', the night before – Coke tins, Fanta bottles, banana skins, sweet wrappers, cigarette butts, and all sorts of other kinds of shit – plus a few newspaper parcels that had come later full of actual shit. When men don't want to stink up their cells during the night by using the toilet they shit in an old *Sunday Muck* and fire that into the yard. That's what these were. All the orderlies took it in turns to do the yard and my turn was due. I'd be out there later.

'PO inspection today,' said Hayes behind.

Harper, the Principal Officer or PO over all of Block 3, was and is a neat freak famous for his rages. If he spots dirt or anything out of order, he lets you have it, both barrels.

'I know,' I said. I turned and went to the wash basin by the door. 'I haven't forgotten.'

'No screw-ups.'

'Don't worry.'

Hayes turned away from my cell door and towards the door of the cell opposite mine. This was Eskimo's. He was the other early bird on 'F' wing. He was a kitchen orderly. He had to get up and away early to get the dinners on the go.

Hayes turned his key in Eskimo's lock and swung his cell door open and clicked Eskimo's door into the keeper.

Eskimo was up. He was in his white Prison Issue or PI scrubs and he was at his wash basin brushing his teeth.

'Morning, Eskimo,' said Hayes.

Hayes set a milk carton on Eskimo's wash basin. Eskimo nodded and gave Hayes the thumbs-up.

'You're welcome, Eskimo,' said Hayes.

Hayes trundled the trolley off to continue his milk run, heading away from the circle. The wheels squeaked. He started to sing, 'It's a Long Way to Tipperary.' Hayes often sings at this hour and he sings well and I like to hear him though I have never mentioned this to him. It would ruin my reputation with the other cons.

I worked my shaving brush on my Palmolive shaving stick. Hayes stopped at the next set of cell doors and hung a carton from the handle. He pushed the trolley forward, and sang on.

I looked across. 'Morning, Eskimo,' I called.

I spread soapy lather on my cheeks.

Eskimo's mouth was full of toothpaste froth. He bent over his sink. He spat. He straightened. 'Morning, Chalky.'

'All right this morning?' I called.

Eskimo took a slug of water from a plastic bottle and began to rinse. You can't drink the water from the taps in the cells. It comes from a storage tank where it might have sat for years and so it's brown and it makes you sick. It's prison policy not to let us have mains. Their thinking is this: a man barricades himself in his cell and only has the brown water to drink is going to surrender far quicker than the man with mains coming out of his wash basin tap.

Eskimo spat into his sink.

'I'm okay, yeah, I'm okay,' he called back.

He was a thin, stringy fellow with a big sharp nose and small dark eyes and shiny, oily skin and absolutely huge hands.

Eskimo was a lifer. He'd broken into a house in the middle of the night because he thought the householder, a grandmother in her eighties, had a fortune under her mattress. She didn't of course. They never do.

When she heard him the old woman woke up and got out of bed and came out of her bedroom and met Eskimo on the landing. He hit her on the head with the hammer he had brought along. He hit her many times. He killed her. After he left the house he threw the hammer into a hedge. It had his blood and sweat on it. That's how they got him. They found the hammer and worked from there. He'd been in prison before so his details were in the police system.

When he first arrived at Loanend everybody called him 'Basher Quinn'. Lurid articles about him and what he done from the *Sunday Muck* newspaper were stuck to his cell door along with crude drawings of a stickman swinging from a gallows with 'Rot in Hell Basher Quinn' scrawled below.

Because of his crime a lot of cons had it in for him but somehow he escaped a tanking. Then he got his job in the kitchen where another orderly, who liked his Dylan, remembered 'The Mighty Quinn (Quinn the Eskimo)' and gave him his new nickname. He stopped being Basher, became Eskimo instead, and his life looked up.

What couldn't be changed though was him. What he was. His nature. Eskimo was a compulsive liar. He fibbed about anything and everything: the cars he had owned, how much booze he could put away, the girls he had fucked and the cash he'd splashed about when he'd been at large. Some cons found his bollocks amusing and would ask daft questions to egg him but I wasn't one of them. I hate blowhards, and I hated Eskimo's boastings but I kept my feelings hidden.

'Eskimo?' I said nicely.

'Yeah?'

'Any chance of some decent wee rolls?'

We mostly get sliced white on the wings so brown rolls are a much sought-after treat.

'I'll give it a go,' he said. 'A man of my talent should be able to fix you up.'

Eskimo was allowed to bring leftover food back from the kitchen. It was the main perk of the job.

'Your place in heaven's guaranteed,' I said.

'Ta.' Eskimo dried his mouth and folded his towel and draped it neatly over the hot pipe that ran along under the cell window. Then he gave his Chelsea FC duvet cover that was stretched tightly over his bed another tug and made it even tighter and smoother. His bed, like his whole cell, was so immaculate you could've put it in a shop window and sold it. In fact his cell was so impressive the Number One Governor often brought visitors over to see Eskimo's cell with its Chelsea scatter cushions and blue curtains and alphabetically arranged CD rack and open wardrobe with all Eskimo's clothes, immaculately ironed, hanging inside. 'The model cell of a model prisoner,' the Number One liked to tell visitors.

Eskimo hurried off to work. Hayes passed, pushing the trolley, still singing, heading back for the circle, and I shaved and brushed my teeth and got dressed. Then I stepped out. I looked up and down the wing. There was milk hanging on the handle of every cell door. It was something I liked seeing and believe me there isn't much you like to see in jail. It reminded me of my childhood, seeing the milk bottles on the doorsteps of the terraced streets in the early mornings in Belfast. I liked the order, everything ready for the day.

I went up to the circle and over to the class office door. The bottom half was closed but the top was open and the sign was still there Sellotaped to the back that I'd seen the day I arrived: 'The answer is NO! Now what is the question?'

'Ah ha,' I said, addressing Hayes, who was at the counter, writing in the logbook. 'If the answer's no, you don't want the breakfast then.'

'Chalky, you make the same pathetic joke every morning,' said Hayes, 'and it's boring, mate.'

'Is it? I thought you liked my jokes.'

'Shut up and get cooking.'

'Yeah, and look sharp,' said Murray from behind the desk. The two other Day screws sat on the greasy easy chairs. One was Thomas, so everybody called him Tank, and the other, Ben, was known as Big Ben.

I opened the bottom door and went in and made the screws their breakfasts on the Baby Belling cooker in the corner. This isn't popular with everyone. A few of my fellow cons say I should be ashamed of myself and the cunts should make their own fucking breakfasts, and too much time in the company of screws will turn me tout if it hasn't already. But do I care? Do I fuck! I can trade a breakfast when I acquire one as I do from time to time for a fiver in tobacco or phone cards, and what I overhear gives me power and in jail you can never have enough of that. So as far as I'm concerned, the moaners can fuck off.

After the breakfasts, I cleaned the landings and the ablutions, and then, as expected, I was given disposable latex gloves, a spade, a brush and a heavy duty plastic bag and sent to the yard. As well as cans, bottles, bread scraps, fag butts and the rest there were three turd rolls. Inspection then at eleven-thirty. Harper saw nothing that annoyed him and went back to his office without shouting. Result.

A few minutes after the inspection finished the dinners came over from the kitchens in dixies and I dished them out from the tiny servery opposite the class office.

We were locked at twelve-thirty and unlocked at two. I did laundry in the afternoon. The washing machines are in a room off the circle opposite the class office. I do all the clothes on 'E' and 'F' wings and there's always washing to do because there are thirty-six cons. All the other stuff, the heavy stuff, the duvet covers and the towels and so on, go to the prison laundry in a different part of the jail. There are industrial machines over there that are able to handle the weight.

I dished up the teas at four – grey fish in brown batter and dry mushy peas and soggy chips and a choc-ice on a stick. I got back to my cell just before the four-thirty lock-up and found a bag of brown bread rolls on my bed.

'Eskimo,' I shouted, darting out of my cell, 'I'll remember you in my prayers . . .'

I ducked into Eskimo's cell and was surprised to find Eskimo peeling the Chelsea FC cover off his duvet. He was being watched from the corner by Tiny. Tiny was small and stocky and muscular with a square head and a beard that was long and thick like the Birds Eye sea captain's. Tiny's main activities before he came to jail were boozing and joyriding. There was a lonely old man on his estate who used to let Tiny and his mates party in his house. One night the drink ran out and the old man went to bed. Tiny, who was pissed, got it into his head that the old man had more booze hidden somewhere. He went up and woke him. The old man told Tiny he'd no drink and to fuck off. Tiny was raging. He ran to the shed in the garden because he knew there was a hatchet there that the old man used to cut his kindling for the fire. Tiny grabbed the hatchet and ran back upstairs and hit the old man with it and he didn't stop till the old fellow wasn't moving, or breathing. Then he hid the hatchet in his girlfriend's hot press and went out for a drive in a stolen car. At his trial Tiny claimed the old man had tried to touch him up and in his panic he'd fetched the hatchet and hit him a couple of times in order to show he wasn't queer. He got eighteen years and the girlfriend got five. Since coming to jail he'd found God and was thick with the minister who he'd conned into thinking he was a good-living Christian even as he and his best mate, Red Ken, were dealing drugs – to Eskimo, among others. I liked Tiny even less than Eskimo. Eskimo at least would do you the odd favour. Tiny wouldn't do anything for anybody. He just looked out for himself.

'All right, Tiny?' I said.

I was always careful and pleasant and polite with Tiny because if you annoyed him you got his mate Red Ken too and two against one were odds that didn't interest me.

'Yeah, sweet, and you, Chalky, how's it hanging?' asked Tiny.

'I've no complaints.'

'That's good,' said Tiny, 'because who'd listen to you anyway?'

I said nothing.

'No one likes a whinger, Chalky.'

Was this an observation about whingers in general or me in particular? I couldn't work it out. This was typical of Tiny, and Red Ken for that matter – you never quite knew where you were with them.

The Chelsea FC duvet cover was off. The matching pillowcase followed. Eskimo bundled everything together and threw it all to Tiny.

'Thanks, mate,' said Tiny. He slipped past me and left the cell. He was on 'E' wing, the other wing. His cell was next door to Red Ken's.

'Eskimo, why'd you give wee Tiny your duvet and pillowcase?' I asked.

'I don't want them,' said Eskimo.

I didn't believe him. Eskimo loved his Chelsea FC stuff. He was mad for it.

'Could you get me a new bedding set from the store?' he asked. He sounded miserable.

'Yeah, sure.'

In the store I found a PI duvet cover and pillowcase. They were a faded green from endless boiling in the prison laundry. I brought them back to Eskimo.

'Lock-up,' I heard a screw shouting on the wing.

'Thanks, Chalky,' Eskimo said as he took the bedding. His voice wavered as he said this. I thought he was going to cry or kiss my hand and I wasn't certain which would be worse.

The next evening I was lying on my bed during association when I noticed Tiny and Red Ken slipping into Eskimo's cell. Red Ken was a fitness fanatic with a long face and a mouth of enormous teeth. He looked a bit like a horse, and a fucking ugly one at that. He was another lifer. His parents divorced when he was a teenager and his father married a woman who was only a few years older than Ken was. Ken was staying at his father's one weekend and he necked a bottle of vodka and then he stabbed his father and the new young wife to death while they slept in bed together. He only stabbed his father a few times and just in the neck but he stabbed the young wife many times all over her body and he only stopped stabbing her, according to the papers, when the knife broke inside her. Tiny is his best friend in prison. Together, Tiny and Red Ken are known as the Evil Twins.

I pretended to read a John Grisham novel while watching Eskimo's door. After a moment the Evil Twins emerged carrying the set of Chelsea FC scatter cushions from Eskimo's bed that matched the duvet and pillowcase Tiny'd already taken. Eskimo had gotten special permission from security to have these because of the one pillow per cell rule. This is apparently because you need two pillows or more to suffocate somebody. If I'd believed the duvet and pillowcase was a one-off, now I knew better, except I hadn't thought it a one-off. Eskimo was in debt for drugs. He was giving the Evil Twins what he owned to pay it off. That's what this was.

Over the following weeks the Evil Twins carried away the rest of Eskimo's Chelsea FC stuff. Then they had his curtains and his DVD player and his DVDs and his CDs and his console and all his console games until his cell was bare except for the basic PI furniture of bed, wardrobe, table, chair, and a religious calendar that Tiny gave him. Next they took all his clothes including his Chelsea FC strip and his Converse trainers and Eskimo was reduced to wearing his kitchen scrubs all the time, white overalls with PI in indelible red ink on the cuffs and turn-ups, plus the heavy waterproof boots issued to all kitchen orderlies. I wasn't the only one who noticed the changes. One morning when I was shaving I overheard Hayes asking Eskimo where all his stuff had gone and Eskimo said he didn't follow Chelsea anymore and he wanted a clean empty cell, plus he was happy wearing his scrubs and boots every day, and Hayes, knowing he'd hit a wall and he wasn't going to get any change out of Eskimo, left it at that.

It was after overhearing this that I decided. I didn't like Eskimo and he wasn't very likeable but he was being bullied and I hated that. The very least I could do was to have a word. Even a tosser like Eskimo didn't deserve this.

I waited till the next Saturday evening. The unlock for evening asso came at five-thirty and as soon as the doors opened I slipped across the corridor and went into Eskimo's cell and found him sitting on his bed.

'Eskimo,' I said.

'Chalky.' He sounded nervous.

I knew at once what was wrong. Just for a moment as I came in and before he saw who I was, he'd thought I was Tiny or Red Ken.

'Look, mate,' I said. 'I'm gonna come right to the point. You need to tell somebody about what's happening.'

I didn't need to say more. He looked at me. He knew I knew and he knew I knew he knew. He couldn't pretend it wasn't happening anymore, whatever it was exactly.

Eskimo puffed up his pockmarked cheeks and blew out. 'Oh yeah, and become a tout,' he said. 'I'd be battered worse than the kiddie-fiddlers if I did that.'

'I could say something when I'm making the screws' breakfasts,' I said. 'Just drop a hint – nobody'd know where it came from.'

'Don't even think about it.'

'Well, is there anything I can do?'

He got off the bed, lifted the mattress up and pulled a CD out.

'I wasn't gonna let the Evil Twins have this,' he said. 'Will you keep it for me?'

He handed me *Céline Dion's Greatest Hits.* After Chelsea FC she was his greatest passion.

'Sure. Any time you wanna hear it, just come over to my cell. We'll bang it on.'

He smiled weakly and his eyes filled with tears. I carried his CD across and put it with mine.

Now here's the thing. Even though they'd taken everything he had the Evil Twins kept visiting Eskimo during evening asso over the following weeks. And I noticed when they did they always closed the door over after them. Cons are allowed to do this if they want a bit of privacy. And as time wore on Eskimo lost weight and looked more and more wasted and depressed.

I was crossing the circle heading for the laundry room when I spotted the Evil Twins outside the class office. Each carried a Loanend Suitcase full of his clothes and each looked really fucked off. I was delighted. I stopped.

'Gentlemen,' I said. 'Are you leaving us?'

'What does it fucking look like?' said Red Ken.

'We're going to the block,' said Tiny.

He meant the Punishment Block though technically it is known as the Good Order Unit, the GOU, an acronym even the screws can't bring themselves to use. Riot screws, tough guys who wear boiler suits instead of uniforms, run the Punishment Block and it is a place to be avoided. No one has a good time over there.

Over the following days the story emerged via the bush telegraph. Eskimo owed the Evil Twins for drugs. He couldn't pay them so they took everything he owned. But that still wasn't enough so then he'd had to provide the Evil Twins with hand jobs and blow jobs and God only knows what other kinds of dirty old jobs. Eskimo eventually broke and blabbed to his probation officer. His probation officer told security. Security ordered that the Evil Twins should be moved from 'E' wing to the Punishment Block pending inquiries.

But, being the cunning little cunts that they were, the Evil Twins knew exactly how the system worked and exactly how to play it. As soon as they were told what they'd been accused of they made counter allegations. They said it wasn't them who'd preyed on Eskimo. It was Eskimo who'd preyed on them. This was bollocks but they knew the protocol in HMP Loanend. When prisoners make complaints against one another all have equal status and all have to be treated the same and investigated. Now because they'd been accused first the Evil Twins still had to go to the Punishment Block while Eskimo would be left on 'F' wing but other than that there was no difference between them. The Evil Twins were entitled to be treated as victims as much as Eskimo was until the truth was established. And they'd a lot of sympathy. A lot of cons chose to believe the Evil Twins' stupid story. Oh yes, they said, Eskimo was the bastard and Tiny and Red Ken were his victims. It was nonsense but by choosing to believe it, cons could avoid annoying two of the jail's main dealers. As for the prison governors, they couldn't afford to be seen to take sides even though they knew the Evil Twins were the culprits. So they played it by the book and set about investigating both sets of allegations impartially.

As the investigations ground on the Twins put the word out and their friends did the rest. Things got ugly for Eskimo. Graffiti reading 'Basher Quinn is a tout' and 'K.A.T' – short for Kill All Touts – appeared on his cell door. It was like the early days again when everybody hated him because he'd killed a lovely old granny. So he withdrew from prison life. He'd no option. Other than when he was in the kitchen where he was safe enough, Eskimo now opted to be locked in his cell all the time and he never came out for association.

But no matter the precautions you take, when you fuck off the likes of the Evil Twins, you're screwed. You see they have to act against you if you've fucked them because then every con will know what will happen if you fuck with them, whereas not to act would send out the opposite message and then no one would respect them anymore and their drug dealing biz would go tits up and they'd be ruined. The Evil Twins couldn't be having that, no way.

This was how they did it. The Twins were still in the Punishment Block and they were still dealing. They picked a couple of clowns in Block 3 and let them run up huge drug debts. Then the Evil Twins sent some friends who were outside to visit the families of the clowns at their homes. The friends brought a message. If the drug debt the clowns had rung up in Loanend wasn't paid immediately then things were going to get messy for the families outside. On the other hand, if the clowns were prepared to do a little job, their debts would be written off completely. The families told this to the clowns on their next prison visit and, as arguments went, it was irresistible. The job, of course, was Eskimo.

The two clowns caught him on the front stairs that connect the big Recreation Hall downstairs with 'C', 'D', 'E' and 'F' wings on the first floor. They picked the part of the front stairs that the camera doesn't cover and they got him as he was coming back from the kitchen one afternoon. It seems one of them held him down and the other one cut his throat with a knife that'd been smuggled in. Afterwards the word went out. Touts beware. Grass the Evil Twins up and this was what you got.

Once the police forensics had been in and done their stuff and they'd carted Eskimo's body away, I was sent to the stairwell to clean up. I was the 'E' and 'F' wing orderly. It was my call. That's what I did. I cleaned.

I'd only a toothbrush for the job and the dirty mess of dry blood was like old brown glue. It took a long time and a lot of effort to get it shifted but I got the job done and that should have been that. End of story. It wasn't though.

With Eskimo gone they couldn't keep the Twins in the Punishment Block anymore, so they let them out. They had to. They returned to Block 3, crowing. That turned my stomach.

As for the clowns, they were eventually fingered and brought to trial. They'd been bought off and they had a brilliant barrister, all arranged by the Twins' friends. As instructed, they each said the other had the knife and they were just the lookout and as the prosecution didn't know who had done what both were convicted in the end on lesser charges. They only got a few years each.

I still have Eskimo's Celine Dion CD. I'm not a fan but now and again I give it spin and whenever I do the same thoughts always come to me – in comparison to Eskimo I've got off pretty light with twelve years. I like to feel sorry for myself as much as the next man, so it does me good to be reminded there are others who've had it far worse.

Chums

Jail friendships aren't proper friendships. How can they be? You don't get to pick your fellow cons. The judge does that and you just have to get on with whoever he decides to throw in prison along with you.

And whatever we might say while we're in jail, we all know it's very unlikely that we'll seek our jail friends out after we leave. We also know that if we ever do run in to somebody we know from the jail on the outside – and chances are we will – we'll probably just nod at each other and pass on. Once you're out you never want to revisit the place, even if it's just in conversation.

This is what I believe anyhow and it works for me. I get on the best I can in prison and I tell myself when I'm finished I'll put it all behind me. I won't be turning round like Lot's wife to look.

There's just one problem with all this. Sometimes in jail you find yourself liking another prisoner and knowing you might meet up on the outside and when this happens you can't help yourself.

Victor McGloyn ran with a north Belfast gang called the Glengormley Terrors. Two days after his sixteenth birthday Victor killed a wee lad from a rival gang with a samurai sword he'd got off eBay. The tabloids said he cut his victim's head off but that was crap. Victor just severed the jugular and the poor wee lad bled to death on the Diamond in the Rathcoole estate.

Victor was sentenced to be detained at Her Majesty's Pleasure – the equivalent of a life sentence for a juvenile – and he started his sentence in Her Majesty's Young Offenders' Centre, Culcavy. Once he turned twenty-one he was shipped up to Loanend and allocated to 'E' and 'F' wings, my patch. We both sized one another up and we both realised pretty quickly it'd be mutually beneficial to get along. He guessed I'd a certain amount of influence and I'd steer him right and I'd even speak up for him if necessary. For my part I suspected he was naïve and pliant and would be useful. So I helped him to find his feet. I told him who was who. I introduced him to one or two other guys. We got along. Then Victor got a job in the Tuck Shop and it wasn't long before I had him stealing sugar for our resident hooch maker, and I can tell you stealing the amounts Victor did took courage *and* ingenuity.

But self-interest wasn't my sole motive no matter how much I tried to pretend otherwise. Victor reminded me of my younger stupider self. He also had a good eye, and I liked that. He could do stuff. For twenty-five grams of tobacco he'd copy in pencil any photograph you wanted and it'd be a damned fine copy. For a tenner's worth of phone cards he'd knock you up in acrylic paint the crest of your football club or your paramilitary grouping or a cartoon character. And for a quarter of blow or a wrap of Subutex he'd paint you a lovely wee Irish thatched cottage complete with donkey, cart and colleen. Yes, it was jail art, but it was high-end jail art. If Victor had been born into a different class and had a different education then he'd have done something and he'd have become somebody. But he was what he was and that was a thug, albeit a talented one. I told him to join Mrs Cartmill's art class. He did.

He hadn't been with Mrs Cartmill long when one of the Governors pitched up with a request. The jail was redoing the Visitors' Centre where prisoners met their families. Paintings were needed to hang on the newly painted walls. The Governor didn't want anything contentious like portraits of Bobby Sands or nudes copied from *Readers' Wives* so they came up with the brilliant idea that all the paintings had to be copies of classics.

As Victor was the star of Mrs Cartmill's class, he was asked to do one of these. It was good to be asked. He was chuffed about that. But it was also what would happen that pleased him. He knew when the finished paintings officially went up in Visits there'd be a do to celebrate. It would be attended by Governors and screws and assorted do-gooders and the contributors' families. That meant Victor could invite his ma and when she saw his canvas hanging up she'd realise he wasn't all bad. That was another thing about Victor. He wasn't bothered about his crime and the wee lad he'd killed but he was dead worried about the pain he'd caused his ma by what he done and her now being left on her own because he was in jail. You see Victor loved his ma because it had only ever been her and him and he wanted her to know he had a good side too and when she saw his painting in Visits she'd see that.

So Victor got a clutch of art books and began searching but he couldn't find anything suitable to copy and that was when Edmund Hartick got six years for VAT evasion and moved onto 'F' wing.

Edmund had a mansion in Hillsborough stuffed with antiques and paintings that were all in the wife's name to stop the Criminal Assets people taking them. He styled himself as a connoisseur and had a lot of art books in his cell.

One evening Victor appeared at Edmund's cell door and asked to look at Edmund's books.

'Okay,' said Edmund.

Victor went into Edmund's cell and began leafing through his books. The third was the guide from the National Gallery in Dublin and in there Victor found what he wanted. This painting showed a woman with a red shawl in a funny wee white cap seen sideways on. It was *La Jeune Bretonne* by Roderic O'Connor.

'Can I have the lend of your book so I can copy this painting?' asked Victor, showing Edmund the page.

'Nope,' said Edmund.

Victor explained his situation. He had to copy a classic. He'd searched high and low and now he'd finally found it – this one of the woman in the wee hat. He'd a canvas primed and ready in his cell. He could start immediately.

'And I'll look after your book, promise,' Victor said. 'No harm will come to it and I'll have it back to you in a week.'

'No,' said Edmund, 'it doesn't leave the cell.'

Victor pleaded but Edmund wouldn't budge. Victor fetched me into the cell to argue his case. I said to Edmund that Victor was a responsible fellow and he'd look after the book properly and it'd be returned in the same condition as when it was borrowed. I gave my word and Victor offered to leave a surety of tobacco or phone cards or anything Edmund wanted. But still Edmund said no. This was his book and he was under no obligation to lend it and so no, he wouldn't let Victor take it. It stayed in his cell and that was that.

Victor wrangled with Edmund for another couple of minutes and then he stormed out of the cell. I followed him out onto the wing.

'It's a famous painting,' I said. 'Mrs Cartmill will get you a copy.'

'Hartick's a cunt,' said Victor. 'I'll fix him.'

I was in the class office cleaning the Baby Belling stove a couple of days later when Edmund Hartick came to the door.

'I want to report a crime,' he said.

'Well you're in the right place then,' said Hayes. 'What is it?'

'Victor McGloyn wanted the loan of a book of mine. I refused. Now he's stolen it.' Edmund saw me then and called over. 'Hey, Chalky, you were there, in my cell, you know all about this. Tell Mr Hayes about it, Chalky, Victor wanting my book, me saying no, and then him taking the hump. It was my book. I was within my rights to say no . . .'

Victor's cell was searched. The search team didn't find Edmund's book but they did find ecstasy. Victor was charged and got a fortnight in the Punishment Block and before he came back Edmund was moved to another block in case McGloyn wanted to have a go at him.

Time passed. Now he was back, Victor stayed in his cell a lot. He said he was working on his canvas for the Visitors' Centre but he wouldn't let me see.

One morning I saw him in the circle.

'Victor,' I said, 'are you painting that woman in the funny wee white hat seen sideways on by any chance?'

He shrugged.

'Well if not then what are you painting?'

'You'll just have to wait till it goes up,' said Victor.

That's what he told everybody.

Then came the day of the do with all the paintings painted by prisoners from all over Loanend finally on public display. I wasn't there because I wasn't invited but

I did ask somebody who was to take a look and see what Victor had painted. He promised he would but in the event he was so busy scoffing sausage rolls he didn't look at the paintings at all so he couldn't tell me when he came back.

One afternoon, a few days later, the klaxon sounded. You hear this throughout Loanend as opposed to the ordinary alarm bells which just sound in the Blocks. They only set it off if they think something big is about to go off and once the klaxon goes the whole prison is locked automatically. As Hayes was about to close my door I asked what was happening and he told me someone had kicked off in the Visitors' Centre but that was all he knew. Half an hour later the all clear sounded. I was unlocked. The dixies with our tea came over. I dished the food up. There was talk in the queue about what had happened and one of the guys in the queue, who'd been in Visits in the afternoon, said it was Hartick who'd started it. He'd gone psycho, first thrown coffee at a painting and then punched the canvas, making several holes. It being Visits a squad of the Riot screws were waiting outside and they charged in within seconds, wrestled him to the ground, got him in a lock and carted him to the Punishment Block, and because it had happened in Visits they sounded the klaxon. Obviously the cons listening in the queue wanted to know what this was about. Why had Hartick gone ape? The eyewitness couldn't say but I'd an idea.

The next day I was in the laundry room when I heard Hayes bellow, 'McGloyn.'

I saw Victor go into the class office. A moment later I heard a howl of anguish. It was horrible, like an animal dying. Then Victor rushed back out of the class office, bolted down the wing and juked into his cell. He was still howling. Hayes followed him all the way to his cell door.

'Lock me,' Victor shouted from inside his cell and Hayes obliged.

I waited about five minutes and then I went to Victor's door and lifted the flap and looked through the Judas slit. Through the thick glass I saw Victor on his bed. He was sobbing.

'Victor,' I said, 'what is it?'

'My painting in the Visitors' Centre,' he said. 'That cunt Hartick destroyed it.'

The next morning Victor wouldn't go to work and stayed locked. Hayes called me into the class office.

'Chalky,' he said, 'I've a question for you.'

'Go on,' I said, 'though I won't promise to answer.'

He pointed at the big canvas leaning against the wall. Even though it was holed in several places, I could see it was *La Jeune Bretonne* by Roderic O'Connor and it was pretty good, or had been. It had just come over from the Visitors' Centre.

'Did Hartick do that because Victor nicked his book?'

Of course he did but I wasn't about to say so.

'No idea,' I said.

'Victor paid for the frame and the canvas and the paints with his own money, did you know that?'

'No.'

'The Governor's fund would have paid but he said no. He wanted to take the painting home when he left, to his ma, so he was paying in order it would remain his property.'

'Right.' I hadn't known that but it made sense. He'd have wanted his painting over the fire in his ma's house.

'Well, now it's been ruined, Victor doesn't want it, does he?'

'Is that a question or a statement of fact?'

'What do you think? I asked, he doesn't want it, so bin it.'

I began to pull the canvas off the frame. It was like pulling a chicken apart.

'"Welcome to the house of pain,"' I said.

'Where's that from?' asked Hayes.

'It was on the wall of my first-ever cell.'

'How old were you?'

'Fifteen I think.'

'And you thought it meant physical pain but now you're wiser you know we do fifty-seven varieties in jail?'

'Aye.'

I broke the frame and put everything into a black bag.

'It weren't bad what he painted by the look of it,' I said, which it wasn't.

'Your point?' said Hayes.

'I like Victor and I feel sorry for him, you know?'

41

'Chalky, said Hayes, 'don't try to be nice, or chummy. It doesn't suit you. Stick to being a worm. Now fuck that rubbish bag down to the bin, there's a good boy. I don't want it lying about here in case McGloyn sees it and goes off on one. Go on, chop, chop.'

Clusterfuck

Sol's story started outside where all jail tales begin and came to an end of sorts in Cell 14 beside me. I wrote it down.

It was a Monday, early June. In the kitchen of Smyth's, the Belfast Bookmakers, two men sat on late lunch.

Sol, forty-four, with a long face, a small mouth and a chin with a dimple that he hated, was rooting in his lunchbox for the treat his wife, Iris, would have included. Sol found it and pulled it out.

'Ah, Twix again,' said Maurice, the other man.

Maurice pointed at the single finger in its shiny wrapper that Sol was holding. Maurice was sixty, had a grey face and small nasty brown eyes, and looked a bit like a ferret, Sol thought.

'Strictly speaking that can't be a Twix, you know, not if it's just one finger.'

'Why not?'

'Cos Twix is two in Latin.'

Maurice was a twat but Sol never argued with him. When Sol was in prison, as he had been several times earlier in his life, he'd learned, if nothing else, to get along with just about anyone.

'Twix isn't Latin. It's a made-up word, mate.'

Sol tore the end off the sleeve and pulled out the brown-veined bar.

'Like a small penis, isn't it?' said Maurice.

'No,' said Sol calmly.

'So, best moment of the day then?'

'What?'

'When you put that in your mouth?' said Maurice.

'Maurice,' said Sol, 'I'm not going to dignify that with a response.'

Sol bit the end off the bar. For a moment the chocolate and biscuit crumbled, melted and spread through his mouth. Then he felt a sharp pain.

'Christ!' Sol dropped the Twix and put his hand up and touched the upper row of teeth through his right cheek.

'What is it?' said Maurice.

Sol screwed up his face. 'Sore tooth.'

Sol began to probe with his tongue. His wisdom tooth and the next one along were fine but when Sol touched the third, a really big one that he had a vague memory had been drilled and filled years before in a procedure that had lasted an entire afternoon, a line of pain shot from his gum to his cheekbone.

'Jesus!'

'Which one?' asked Maurice.

'The big one, top right, halfway along.'

'Oh, I had that one out.'

Maurice tugged at the side of his mouth to reveal long yellow teeth and the stretch of red, wet gum where the tooth had been. The sight was faintly obscene.

'When the dentist yanked it out,' Maurice continued, 'the nerve came too. It was a big worm, all white and bloody, as long as your hand.'

'I don't want to know,' said Sol.

Maurice looked like he was about to stand. Sol hoped he was going. But instead he leaned forward.

'Listen, mate,' said Maurice. 'I don't suppose you'll be wanting the rest of your Twix, will you?'

That was pure Maurice.

'No, mate, help yourself.'

'Cheers.' Maurice popped the stub into his mouth. 'Lovely,' he said.

Maurice left. Sol rinsed his mouth with warm salt water and went down to the betting shop below. Gavin, the manager, gave him two Panadol. He went to his station and started work. The pain receded. Sol took another two Panadol at the end of the afternoon. By the time Sol stepped into his house that evening, the pain was hardly noticeable. Sol could live with it. Sol closed the front door behind.

'Is that you?' Iris called, as she always did.

'I don't know,' Sol shouted back, which was how he always replied.

Sol went into the kitchen where Iris was making their tea.

'Good day?' asked Iris.

'Yeah, all right, just a bit of toothache.' Sol touched the tooth through his cheek.

'Nasty?'

'Well it was, not so bad now.'

Sol's second wife had a lot of wayward blonde hair and very blue watery eyes and wore a gold chain with a sovereign attached around her neck.

'You should see the dentist,' Iris said. 'Cup of tea?'

'Why not?'

Iris swirled the kettle around to check it had water and pressed the switch, then she kissed him on the top of his head the way his mother would when Sol was a boy and he got in from school.

In the kettle the water started bubbling.

Sol slept surprisingly well that night. The next morning he felt only a twinge in the tooth. Still, he decided to be careful. At breakfast, Sol took his toast without jam and chewed it on the left-hand side of his mouth. His plate cleared, Sol drained his teacup and stood.

'I know you won't,' said Iris, 'so I'll ring the dentist for you.'

Iris sat on the other side of the table eating bran flakes, naked under her quilted dressing gown. Iris never wore anything in bed. She did not even own a nightdress. Sol, on the other hand, always slept in pyjamas, a habit he had acquired when he was a working criminal and the police would frequently raid the house where he lived with his first wife, Betty, and their kids, in the early morning.

'I don't know if I really need to,' Sol said. He touched the tooth through his cheek. 'Seems okay.'

'No harm Mr Crawford taking a look. Does any time not suit?'

Sol circled the table and considered what to say. Now was the perfect opportunity. Why not tell her? Friday afternoon definitely did not suit. Deek's party started at five and Gavin had said Sol could leave work early that night.

Sol was behind Iris now, looking down on her wild hair. It excited him that she was naked under her dressing gown. He slipped his hands under the lapels and cupped her breasts. They were small but soft and, Sol thought, lovely.

'What are you doing?' Iris said.

Deek's party, he thought, this could be a really good time to get it out of the way.

'Giving you a loving caress.'

'Oh, is that what you call it?' she said, pushing him away, laughing.

No, Sol thought, better leave it for now.

'Right, I'm off.' Sol took his lunch box from the worktop. 'Nice treat in here for me is there?'

'Course,' Iris said. 'Don't I always?'

Sol left the house and closed the front door behind carefully. He went down the path and out the gate, closing it quietly too. Iris had trained him not to bang when he went out of or came in to their house.

It was an awful thing but Sol had to face it: too many short sentences to mention plus a long one of seven for armed robbery, a tough man, good in a scrap, believed by his peers to be fearless, and he was actually frightened of his wife. Thank fuck, Sol thought, no one knew.

All of the day that followed the tooth hardly bothered Sol at all. There was just the odd throb now and again.

Sol left Smyth's in good spirits. On the bus he got his favourite seat at the back. On the journey home he watched the city streaming past, paying particular attention to girls in their summer clothes, their short skirts, their halter necks.

He got out at his stop in the sunshine, and walked round to his street. As Sol stepped into his hall Iris called from the kitchen, 'Is that you?'

'I don't know,' Sol said and closed the door quietly.

His gaze went straight to the hall table, where the phone sat and where Iris did her admin. There was a Post-it with 'Sol dentist' written by Iris in her big looping writing with a big pink tick beside it.

Sol went through to the kitchen. Iris was at the sink, the cold tap running, holding an egg under the streaming water.

'I predict egg mayonnaise for tea,' he said.

Iris snorted and rubbed one of her thin wrists under her nose.

'I got you the five o'clock on Friday,' she said.

As Sol registered the information he felt his stomach going tight. Why was he so lame?

'With the dentist,' Iris added.

The shell of the egg she held came away with a gentle soughing noise.

'What did you say?' Sol spoke in what he hoped was his blankest, most neutral voice.

'Dentist, Friday, five o'clock, last appointment.'

'Oh.'

'You won't have to leave too early so Gavin won't get upset. Aren't you pleased? I thought you'd be pleased.'

Iris added the egg to the plate with the other shelled eggs. Their white flesh was almost blue.

'Ah,' Sol said carefully.

'Your mouth is twitching,' Iris said.

It was. Sol felt it. He attempted a smile to cover it, even though it was too late of course.

'Come on, spit it out,' Iris said.

'I met Deek the other day ...'

Iris knocked an egg smartly against the rim of the stainless steel sink. Sol heard the shell cracking. She knew Deek. He was a retired housebreaker and an old friend of Sol's from prison. Deek was also best man at their wedding.

In his speech, which was all fiction, Deek told the guests that on the stag in Amsterdam, Sol had helped out on a porno called *Ready, Steady, Cock*, which he described as the everyday tale of a lady chef who liked to swallow. Iris was appalled. Deek was one of those men, she decided, and later she told Sol this, who had to pull every occasion down to his own level. Everything he came near he dirtied and she had seen no reason since then to change her opinion.

'Deek's having a few mates over,' Sol continued, 'for a few beers, and a bit of cards. That's on Friday.'

'Is that so?' It was fantastic how much disgruntlement Iris packed into three simple words.

'Yeah,' Sol said, 'and I was thinking of going.'

This was not true. Sol actually felt he must go. His old friends, the ones who'd be there, were whispering that Sol was stuck-up these days. Since he got out of jail and married Iris they reckoned he didn't want to know them. He'd become a snob. That really hurt. At Deek's he planned to show everyone he was still the same old Sol. Iris, of course, hated him to have any contact with the old crowd.

'Haven't seen Deek in ages you know,' Sol said. 'And he is, well, was, no, sort of still is, a friend.'

The last sock of shell came away from the last egg.

'Really?' said Iris.

She dried the egg, put it in the cutter and then folded the wires over. An instant later, the egg was in slices.

'So that's a deal,' he said.

Iris tipped the slices from the cutter into a bowl filled with mayonnaise. Sol noticed their plates with lettuce and beetroot already laid out. He could smell the vinegar the beet had come in, sharp, metallic.

'Really, was that what we were doing?' said Iris. 'Making a deal?'

'About Friday,' said Sol, 'yes, that's what I thought.'

'We haven't negotiated anything,' said Iris. 'I simply told you I made you an appointment on Friday at five with the dentist, and you told me you're going to Deek's instead.'

She sliced the other eggs, brusquely.

'The thing is,' he said, 'Deek's thing starts at five. And if I have a jab my mouth'll be sore and I'll be dribbling. A proper idiot.'

Iris vigorously swirled the egg pieces in the mayonnaise, then sprinkled cayenne pepper on.

'I'm not interested in your party problems,' she said.

He paused to give her the impression he was thinking and then Sol said, 'You're right. Better get the tooth done. I'll call in to Deek's after the dentist, just say a quick hello, then come home straight away.'

They ate with the television on. This saved them having to talk. Iris went to bed first and when Sol followed, a few minutes later, she was on her side, her back turned towards him. He stroked her bare shoulder but Iris did not respond. Sol sighed and noisily turned his back on her.

On Wednesday night when Sol went to bed, he again found Iris with her back turned towards him. He curled around her and pressed against her so she could feel his erection. Iris said nothing. Sol rolled away and went to sleep.

On Thursday night he whispered, 'Will we make love?'

'No thank you,' said Iris.

He went to sleep and dreamt he was in a scout hut with all the employees from Smyth's. They were putting on a pageant and Maurice was king and wore a gold crown. Sol had only a small part. He was Maurice's page and walked behind Maurice holding his cape and he wore white tights.

When Sol woke on Friday morning he found the tooth was hurting just a little more than it had all week. He took two painkillers with his tea at breakfast and several more through the course of the day. When four o'clock came Gavin called out to him, 'Oi, go on, off to your party.'

He went to the toilets to have a pee before he left. Sol found Maurice washing his hands.

'How's that tooth?' Maurice called, grinning into the mirror over the sink.

'Still sore.'

'You want to get that seen to,' said Maurice.

'All right, thank you,' he said. 'And you sound just like Iris by the way.'

'I'm not your wife!' Maurice exclaimed. 'You dirty dog.'

Forty minutes later, Sol stood in front of a thin Victorian house, one of a terrace in a square. There were three steps, bowed like a butcher's chopping board, a black front door and a polished brass sign:

Mr James Crawford, BDS (QUB)

He touched his tooth with his tongue. There was a definite thread of pain but it was, Sol felt, quite bearable. He was keen to see the boys. And fuck it, he didn't want jelly lips.

He turned on the spot and sprang away along the pavement. A pretty girl went by, humming to herself. Suddenly, Sol felt in control and certain of his destiny and his reputation. A few cans and a few hands. He'd a couple of hundred he was willing to lose in his back pocket. He'd his taxi money in his shirt pocket, which he wouldn't gamble. Taxi at eleven. Home by midnight.

He walked round the corner to Eazy Cabs, got into a taxi and gave the driver Deek's address. Then he changed his mind and said, 'Just let me out on the Woodstock, would you?'

The driver eased out into the traffic. Through the window Sol saw the clean summer sky overhead. He felt a surge of confidence and he felt certain he was going to win.

Sol got out on the Woodstock. He bought a litre bottle of vodka and two cartons of orange juice in an off licence. Then he strolled round to Deek's. Coming out from the house he could hear party hubbub, and through the front window he saw people standing about, drinking from cans. Sol went in and made himself a vodka and orange in Deek's kitchen. He circulated then, taking care not only to talk to everyone but also to say something simultaneously funny and flattering to everyone. At seven, made careless by several vodkas, he bit into a carrot stick. The pain in his tooth flared up. He drank several more vodkas. As the hours wore on and he drank more, he forgot about his tooth.

At ten the poker started. The stakes, moderate to begin with, soon rose. Sol didn't do well at the start but nearing eleven things changed. He decided to put off calling a taxi. He did not regret the decision. By midnight he was doing very well indeed. Four hundred so far. Fan-fucking-tastic. After this size of a win, he could weather whatever happened with Iris when he got home.

At some point (he had lost track of time but he had finished the vodka, he knew that, and he had switched to tequila, he knew that too), a row broke out. Someone called Leo (someone he didn't know, one of Deek's friends had brought this man along) accused him of cheating. Sol felt invincible. Leo was a sore loser who needed manners put on him. Sol told Leo to fuck off, got up and went into the garden to take a piss beside the little brown shed. When he finished, Sol found Leo standing behind him. He had not noticed before but Leo was very large and very powerfully built. Sol was also aware of his toothache. The pain was pounding now. Leo was pointing his finger in his face and was agitated. Sol's hand snaked along the side of the shed. He was relieved to find something cold and hard that fitted well in his hand. It felt like a piece of scaffolding. Sol felt safer. He could afford to be unequivocal now.

He pulled the scaffolding bar out and held it like a sword. He wanted to keep the big man at bay. But Leo didn't grasp this. He refused to back off. He was still calling Sol a cheat and now he began to call him a snob. Well, that was it. Sol took a swipe. The bar connected with Leo's head, the side, the temple.

The big man started to buckle. The movement struck Sol as somehow like a genuflection, but one that had gone horribly wrong. Then Leo was on the grass, lying very still, with one leg crooked at an odd angle under the other and Deek was at his side saying 'Easy boy,' and the scaffolding bar was being prised out of his right hand.

The following morning, hungover and dry mouthed, Sol was charged with murder and remanded into custody in HMP Loanend. His tooth by now was raging with pain and a week after he arrived in the jail, the decay was drilled out and the hole was filled. Nine months later he was sentenced to life with a recommendation that he serve a minimum of fifteen years. They put him in Block 3, 'F' wing in the cell next door to mine. We became friends and he would tell me what was happening in his life as it happened. On the minus side, Iris divorced him, taking his money and his house. On the plus side, Betty, the first wife, started coming to visit him. One week, when she didn't have the children, she even mentioned she'd like to try again with him, if he was game. He thanked her – he was genuinely touched – and then he suggested they wait and see what happened when he got out.

Four years into his sentence, Sol woke one morning feeling groggy and tired. He shuffled down to the wing Recreation Room and put two pieces of pan loaf into the toaster on the counter and depressed the lever. As the timing mechanism clicked away, he became aware of a dull pain on the right side of his mouth, the upper gum. Gingerly, he touched the tooth, his Twix tooth as he sometimes thought of it, the big one, the troublesome one. Pain darted across his cheek.

He left the toast cooking and went down to the class office. I was in there at the Baby Belling and so was a young prison officer whom Sol hardly knew called Henderson who was covering for Hayes who was on leave. Henderson was sitting at the slanted counter just inside the door writing something in the logbook.

'Excuse me, officer, I need to see the dentist,' said Sol.

Henderson did not look up. He didn't like being disturbed.

'Toothache, here, this one.' Sol pointed at the tooth. 'I've had trouble with it before. I'm in a lot of pain.'

The logbook rustled as Henderson shifted it slightly.

'And I've got this Open University essay to do for next week,' Sol added hastily. He hoped Henderson was one of the new breed of officer who approved of education. 'I'll never manage it with this pain.'

'The dentist is off,' said Henderson without looking up. 'See the nurse at nine.'

The nurse gave Sol two unbranded painkillers to take that morning and two for the evening. Sol took the second pair at eight, just before we were all locked for the night. That was when I popped my head around his door to see how he was.

'All right?' I said.

'I'm fucking dying,' Sol said.

An hour later he sat on his bed, his tooth screaming, and stared at his essay question:

' "The Colosseum, with its spectacles of cruelty, was where Romans found balm for their considerable grievances and, without its crucial function as a safety valve, Roman society would have been much more volatile, and social agitation much more likely."

'Explore the truth of this statement. Your essay should include reference to and quotation from the Latin texts in your study pack.

Essay length: 1,500 words'

In the corridor outside Sol heard the Night screw's footfalls.

'Excuse me,' Sol called out.

In the post lock-down quiet I could hear Sol's voice. I could hear everything. The Night screw stopped outside Sol's cell door.

'I'm being killed by toothache here,' Sol called, 'you wouldn't have any painkillers, would you?'

'I'll see what I can do.'

The Night screw went away and came back.

'You're in luck,' he said. 'Boots' finest.'

There was a scraping sound in the corridor. I guessed, correctly, that it was the blister pack being pushed under Sol's cell door.

'Thanks, mate,' Sol shouted. 'These are fucking fantastic. They'll do the trick.'

They were branded and very powerful. The real McCoy. No wonder Sol sounded so pleased.

He took two immediately. The pain didn't disappear but it eased. Sol started his essay. He worked on through the night. Every time Sol felt the pain drawing near, he took another tablet and the pain would withdraw. By six the following morning, Sol had a passable first draft written and all the painkillers from the blister pack were gone. When he got into bed Sol heard rooks cawing in the exercise yard. That was the last sound he heard until he was woken, a couple of hours later, by the key turning. The door swung open. He saw Henderson in the doorway.

'What time is it?'

'Eight.'

'I feel terrible.' Sol felt the pain surging out of his bad tooth and up his face. 'Awful toothache.'

'Never mind that,' said Henderson, 'you've been called for a drugs test.'

The Mandatory Drug Test, or MDT, was random and could not be declined.

Sol got up and an Escort screw took him to the testing centre. Inside he was held in a glass-fronted holding cell for an hour, strip-searched, told about the test and the penalties for failure, given a plastic cup and brought to a toilet at the back of room. Here, watched by a Test screw, he pissed in the cup. This done, the cup was capped, bagged and sent off for testing, and Sol was returned to the block.

The next day, Sol was on his bed copying his essay out. His tooth was still aching and he had just taken two more of the unbranded painkillers given out by the nurse that weren't very good. There was still no dentist, though why this was no one had explained. All Sol got when he asked was the standard reply: 'The dentist is off.' But Sol had the essay written and, bad and awful as he felt, he could just about concentrate enough to copy it out.

Henderson appeared in his cell doorway.

'PO Harper wants to see you, now.'

Sol went down the back stairs. Principal Officer Harper's office was on the circle opposite the front door. Harper was sitting behind his desk when Sol went in. He was a dapper man with white hair and a neat goatee beard. Harper was Murray's superior. He was everyone's superior. Harper ran the block.

'You failed,' said Harper.

'What?'

'Your drugs test.'

'That's impossible!'

Sol didn't smoke blow or take E's or trips. Sol didn't do drugs at all. Sol was nearly fifty-one for fuck's sake.

'I don't do drugs. You know that.'

'Codeine,' said Harper, sharply.

'Codeine?'

'That's what the report says.' Harper squinted at the piece of paper in front of him. 'You had codeine in your urine.'

Jesus! The fucking blister pack from the Night screw. Boots' finest. Oh Christ.

'I had toothache the other night and the Night screw gave them to me.'

'It's irrelevant where you got them,' said PO Harper. 'You know the regulations. Codeine is a banned substance unless it's prescribed and, looking at your medical sheet,' he waved another piece of paper, 'I see you've had painkillers for toothache, yes, but there's no codeine on your script. You've fucked up, mate.'

Sol, who was standing, wanted to sit. Sol had worked hard to progress from Basic, his status when he arrived, to Standard, which he rose to, to Enhanced, which he eventually became and which all prisoners wanted to be because of the privileges and perks to which it entitled a man. Now, for having failed the drug test, he would be dropped to Standard. His wage would be slashed. He would be locked at four-thirty. Worst of all, he would lose his video recorder and he needed that to do his OU course. He needed it so he could record the programmes and then replay them and take notes. If he couldn't he was fucked. This was a catastrophe. Sol felt a desperate need to explain and to beg. Sol opened his mouth.

'Don't,' said Harper, 'you know the rules. Drugs, without a script, you're down to Standard, no exceptions. Now go back to your cell, get your head down, get some good reports and work your way back up to Enhanced.'

'There's a programme about the fall of Ancient Rome and the Dark Ages at 2 a.m. tonight that I've got to record for my OU,' said Sol. 'I need to record it so I can make notes from it.'

Sol tried hard to keep the pleading out of his voice but he realised he'd failed. Now he felt like crying.

'I don't give a fuck what you have to do,' said Harper, bleakly. 'You took codeine, no script, now take the consequences. Off you go.'

When Sol got back to his cell he found Henderson was already there. Harper, Sol realised, had phoned his instructions up already. Henderson had already unplugged the video recorder, and now he was folding the wires up. This done, Henderson stuffed the remote and the wires into his pockets, then he picked up the unit and left Sol's cell without a word. Sol sat on his bed.

From the Twix to this, he thought, there was a direct line of connection. That was life. When you got to the end of something it all made sense. If only it was the other way round though, and he could see where something was headed from the beginning. Forward hindsight – wouldn't that be wonderful, he thought.

At that moment, having just seen Henderson coming out with Sol's video recorder, I walked up to Sol's cell door. I stopped. I looked in. Sol, sitting on the bed, looked stooped, crushed, and miserable. He was staring at the space where his video recorder had stood until a few minutes earlier. I went in.

'You all right?' I said.

'No, Chalky,' he said, 'I'm fucked.' Then he shouted, 'It's a clusterfuck, a fucking cunting clusterfuck and I'm completely and utterly fucked.'

Then he said he was going to smash his cell and barricade himself in. They'd have to carry him out in a coffin, he said.

Later, much later, when he'd calmed down, he told me the whole story, from the start in the bookies to the end when he was dropped to Standard. After I finishing writing it down I gave it to him to read. 'Fair enough,' he said, of my account. The events, on the other hand, in the story, they were different, he said. They were a nightmare from which he couldn't wake up.

Smurf

I was sitting in my cell one evening when a figure appeared in my doorway. It was Gilligan. He was called Yogi Bear but I never understood the reason why.

He was bony and round-shouldered and had dark angry eyes and long fingernails on his right hand because he played guitar. He did a good stare. Back in the 1980s he and some Loyalist mates had thrown a Catholic into an oil drum, doused him with petrol, set him on fire and killed him. Very brave that. Yogi was let go after the Good Friday Agreement when all the paramilitaries were let out but he was brought back to Loanend a few years later for a licence breach.

Yogi Bear's explanation for his recall was that he'd had a row with his daughter's boyfriend and chopped off three of his fingers and put them down the waste-disposal unit. What he'd actually done was hit the boyfriend in the eye with a golf club when he was sleeping. The boyfriend lost the eye. Hayes said something to me one time and I've never forgotten it: 'You won't find Yogi Bear scraping the bottom of the barrel. No, to find Yogi Bear you have to lift the barrel up and look in the dirt underneath.'

Yogi Bear wasn't the only paramilitary in the jail. There were about fifty Loyalists and the same number of Republicans. A few were young Turks from the new dissident organisations but most were old-timers like Yogi, let out after 1998 and then brought back on account of doing something stupid involving cars or drink or their poor wives.

'Have you got a wee minute?' asked Yogi Bear.

I wasn't going to say no. Yogi Bear wasn't a man to annoy. It was the company he kept. Piss him off and you'd have to take on not just him but his mates and a war like that, one against fifty, was a war no one could win.

'Sure, come on in,' I said.

He sat on the edge of my bed and turned his face towards me. His right cheek was pink and normal but the left was white and shiny. At some point during his time in jail, some Republicans had cornered Yogi in a Recreation Room where cons cut hair and make toast and iron clothes. They held Yogi down and burnt his face with a hot iron.

'Listen, Chalky,' he began, 'what I'm about to say doesn't go beyond these walls.'

'Sure,' I said.

'We're not happy,' he said. 'Republicans neither.'

That was a first – Yogi Bear speaking warmly about his enemies.

'We want changes,' he said.

'We?'

He nodded.

'You're doing something together?'

He nodded again.

'Is this about segregation?'

'Aye.'

The only cons that were segregated were sex offenders or ex-policemen or ex-soldiers, men the jail said were vulnerable, and who were kept locked twenty-four/seven on the wings or sent across to the Punishment Block and held there. Paramilitaries had been segregated in the past but they weren't anymore and that's what Yogi was getting at. If they could have that again they could pretend the Troubles were back on again and they were POWs.

'We're shutting the jail down,' said Yogi Bear, 'with every man in it, one hundred per cent support. Word'll be passed along to you, the evening before. You don't say a word, not even to another prisoner. You fill your flasks with hot water, and you get some bottles of drinking water in. Then, when you get your unlock the next morning, you just say you're not coming out. Understand?'

I did. I nodded.

'And for the next twenty-four hours, you don't put so much as a foot outside this cell, not for food, water, shower, doctor, dentist, phone, visits, heart attack, nothing. And then the next morning, come unlock, out you go. Got it? All it is, is twenty-four hours when nothing happens – laundry, workshops, kitchen, trades, Education, they're all off. That's how we'll learn them.'

'Learn them what?' I asked.

'They don't run the jail. We do. And we are going to get segregation and we'll keep closing the place down until we do.'

I got my tip-off about the strike from Paddy the Provo. I laid in my water supplies and went to bed. At seven the next morning the door swung back.

'Morning, Chalky,' said Hayes. I wished it were Big Ben or Tank at my door. I didn't like either of them so telling them I wasn't coming out wouldn't worry me. But it was Hayes and now I had to do it.

'I'm not going to work,' I said. 'I don't feel well.'

'You look all right.' Hayes didn't know it was a strike yet so he was pretty reasonable.

'I'm not coming out,' I said.

'Murray won't like it,' said Hayes. 'Who's going to do breakfasts?'

'Maybe Mr Murray?'

'Not funny. You've got a day's work to do. You could get an adverse report for this you know.'

'I'm sick, really.'

'All right, suit yourself,' he said. 'There's your milk.' He put my pint on the wash basin. 'I'll tell Murray you've got syphilis or something.'

He closed the door and turned the key. Then I heard the key in the lock of the cell opposite, Eskimo's old cell, and now the home of Smurf, from his surname, Murphy, a petty criminal (burglary, a bit of fraud, illegal fags, that sort of thing), who was also a kitchen orderly like Eskimo had been.

'Morning, Smurf,' I heard Hayes say.

'Morning. What's with Chalky?' asked Smurf. He saw my cell door wasn't open as usual but closed.

'Oh, claims he's got some lurgy,' said Hayes, 'but he's just skiving. Doesn't want to make the breakfasts and the eejit doesn't know we got in extra bacon and pudding for him this morning to take away.'

'His loss,' said Smurf.

I heard his laughter and then his footsteps on the linoleum as he stepped out of his cell and moved up the wing. The rubber soles of his PI water boots made a sticky sound as he walked. I realised they hadn't told him about the strike. No, of course they wouldn't. Smurf's ma, a Catholic, had been abducted, beaten, shot and buried in a bog by Republicans back in the bad old days and because of that Smurf hated paramilitaries, all kinds not just Republicans, and he also made it his business that everyone knew what he thought about them and that was why they hadn't included him, which was a devious fucking sneaky thing to do because now the poor fucker was about to become something worse than even a tout which was a strike-breaker, only he didn't know it yet. I know, I could've called out, 'Smurf, there's a strike, don't scab, go back to your cell,' but I didn't. Sign my own death warrant by siding with a blackleg? No thank you. I kept my mouth shut and let him walk away.

I lay on stupidly hoping that at eight o'clock come the general unlock one or two others would put their noses outside their cells and that'd be the strike broken, at least on our wing. I decided I'd follow their lead if that happened. It'd start a trend and then the strike would peter out and Smurf might survive. Eight o'clock came. I heard the first key in the first door and the door opening and a burst of talk and then the door closing and being locked again. It was the same story at every cell as every single prisoner on 'F' wing refused to come out on unlock.

Smurf returned at four to calls of 'Scab' and 'Blackleg' and fists drumming on steel doors as he walked down the landing.

The next day when normal regime resumed Smurf knew it was too dangerous for him to go to the kitchen now. He stayed voluntarily locked like that twenty-four hours a day for six weeks waiting for everything to die down. He only ate when the screws remembered to bring him something and he only showered when the screws remembered to bring him out while the rest of us were locked.

Eventually the announcement came through. The prison had agreed. Segregated wings for Loyalists and Republicans would be created.

A wave of euphoria spread through the jail. Even though this new rule only applied to about a hundred-odd paramilitaries and the rest of us, about a thousand Ordinary Decent Criminals, would be unaffected by it, we still felt we'd got something. We still felt we'd beaten the system.

This sense of victory also affected Smurf. It took the sting out of his scabbing, or so he thought, and he felt it was safe to show his face again. He quietly returned to work. The other cons in the kitchen ignored him. That didn't surprise him. But nobody had a go. And nobody gave him lip. In the evenings Smurf stayed locked in his cell at his own request.

A few weeks passed. It wasn't going to happen, I thought, the retribution that a man who'd scabbed could expect and that was good because if it never came then I'd never have to feel bad about what I done, or didn't do.

I was wrong. Nobody forgets, not in jail they don't.

It happened in the kitchens. Two guys did it, freelancers, who weren't put up to it but just did it of their own bat because, as they said later, they couldn't let a scab away with what Smurf done. No way.

They got a mop bucket, the industrial kind, on wheels. Put a gallon of boiling water in. Added sugar.

Smurf was at his work station peeling spuds or something. The mop bucket was trundled up behind him. He thought nothing of it. He thought the floor was being washed. The floor was always being washed in the kitchen. Fucking health and safety.

The two avengers hoisted up the mop bucket and tipped the contents over Smurf's head. A gallon of boiling water, cloudy with sugar. He was drenched. It melted his hair. It split his scalp. It soaked into his scrubs, and his scrubs and his skin sort of melted together. His screams were said to be something terrible.

He collapsed on the floor. A Kitchen screw pressed the bell. No kitchen orderlies moved because none of them wanted to be seen helping a scab except for one, an ex-Loyalist who was in for a domestic and who'd been in the St John's Ambulance once. He got Smurf's scrubs off and covered him in tea towels soaked in cold water to hold the skin on and then he held Smurf in his arms and comforted him until the ambulance came, which took a fucking hour.

Smurf was taken away to hospital. He lived and now the Good Samaritan who saved Smurf became a hate figure. He started finding messages stuck to his cell door. He was a Fenian-loving cunt and he was next. He was pulled from the kitchen and put in the Punishment Block for his own safety.

As for the guys who done the scalding, they were adjudicated at the prison court over in the Punishment Block and got time there. I often wondered if they and the Good Samaritan ever ran into each other. It was possible. They were in the same place.

After the two avengers were let out of the Punishment Block and went back to their wings I'm told they were cheered. Well, they were heroes, weren't they, on account of what they done. I thought otherwise but knew better than to say anything.

Smurf never returned to Loanend. I heard later he went a bit mad and did the rest of his time in a psych ward.

SC

I was locked around eight. The wing fell quiet. Gary the Night screw came on. The Night screw's always alone. One man, two landings. It cuts the costs down. I could tell it was Gary because he's got a bad limp.

The Day screws went off taking all the cell keys with them. The keys are kept in the Central Control Room during the night. If something happens, like a con having a heart attack and needing to go out to hospital, then the Night screw phones Control and the Riot screws from the Punishment Block bring the keys across to the block. It's a right old palaver getting unlocked at night.

That evening I wrote a letter, a wee saucy one. I did it for another con to send out, once he'd recopied it, to his missus. I've a nice wee sideline writing these. For two sides of A4 as long as it's good stuff I get twenty-five grams of Golden Virginia. The prisoner had said his wife liked a sea setting so in this one I gave her one: I had her buck naked at the top of a lighthouse while hubby, who she could hear, was slowly climbing the spiral stairs towards her. It was one of those situations that I could have written ten pages about if I'd had to.

When I'd finished writing I rolled a joint and smoked it by my window. I heard the flap rise. I knew Gary was looking through the glass in the Judas slit to see if I was alive. I paid him no heed. Gary folded the flap down to cover the slit so I couldn't see out and went to the next cell and then the next and when he'd looked in every cell along the wing and checked every con was alive he put a key in the machine at the bottom of the wing and that sent a message to the Control Room to show he'd done his round.

As well as the wee tally machine there was also a camera on the wing. It sent pictures of Gary back to a monitor in the Control Room. A different camera watched Gary when he was back in the class office and those images were also fed back to the Control Room. So Gary was watched all night long by another screw who watched the feeds from all the cameras around the jail over in the Control Room.

And there must be a lot of monitors because there are a lot of cameras, for besides the wings they're also in the Recreation Rooms and the exercise yards and the walkways and the workshops and Education and though they don't cover everywhere they cover a great deal. We all know about them too of course and what they do and we all know where they are and we know what to do in order not to be seen. It is also easy to forget about them because they are pretty small and then they catch you out. Even the screws sometimes forget they're there.

I turned my light off at half-eleven. I was aware of the flap lifting at midnight. Gary turned on my light from the switch outside and looked in and then the light went off. This is what happens every hour through the night, 365 nights of the year, but I never notice once I'm asleep. I'm a good sleeper.

The next day in the afternoon I was in the laundry room. I am never out of that bloody room. The work is never-ending.

I loaded the machine and turned it on. Then I stepped out to the circle and saw an Escort screw arrive with a con in tow. I know plenty of guys but I didn't know this one.

The Escort screw shouted, 'One on!' like they always do though nobody listens. Like so much in jail it's just an old habit, a tradition, and not having a lot of those, the screws insist on keeping this one going.

'Wait here,' said the Escort screw to the con. He pointed at the worn linoleum in front of the hot water boiler we all use to fill our Thermos flasks so we can make tea or coffee or Pot Noodles and the like when we're locked at night.

The Escort screw went into the class office to hand over the man's paperwork. The con dumped his two bulging Loanend Suitcases on the floor. I saw the name written on the side of each Loanend Suitcase in black felt-tip. P. McDowell. His prison number was written underneath. Ah right, I knew who he was now. And I knew his story, all nine yards. It had been in the papers, and there'd been lots of chatter about him too. You study the *Sunday Muck* and talk to other prisoners and you can get the gen on a man's whole fucking life.

McDowell was what you call a revolving door criminal, because he'd been in and out of jail all his life. It was always for small stuff like taking and driving away or drunk and disorderly or shoplifting – that kind of thing. He was a boring fellow and he'd no real personality and he wasn't really liked or disliked. He was the kind of bloke you'd hardly notice, pretty unremarkable.

Before I saw him on the circle he'd been out in the world for a few years. He'd done okay. He'd kept out of trouble. He'd found love – or the next best thing anyway: a woman with children who welcomed him into her bed and they'd had more children. They lived in a Housing Executive house on an estate outside Belfast. They survived on benefits and spent their days getting blocked as often as they could afford the drink and then scrapping. They were always knocking lumps out of one another. They were like something off *The Jeremy Kyle Show*.

Then one evening they had the mother of all rows after a day on the piss. She accused him of having another woman. He denied it. She got stuck into him. There was a lot of slagging. He stormed out of the house. She charged out after him.

The row continued first in the front garden and then on the pavement beyond. The neighbours heard. They all piled out to gawp and add their tuppence worth.

The argument went on for a while until McDowell decided he'd had enough. He lurched towards his car parked by the kerb.

'Don't get in,' she shouted.

'Away to fuck with you,' he replied.

'Stop acting the cunt and get inside,' she shouted.

He shrugged. She lunged after him in the hope of holding him back. She got ahold of him. She pulled. He pushed. She fell. He got in his motor. He sped away. The crowd muttered. 'No call for that, you don't push a woman around, you ignorant bastard.'

Somebody lifted his woman to her feet. She staggered out into the middle of the road.

'Come back,' she cried in the direction of the vanished car.

The crowd offered advice. 'Come on girl, you're better off without him. Get inside, get a drink down you.'

Nobody noticed with all this slabbering. McDowell had stopped the car and turned around. He was driving back. And the trouble was the girlfriend was still there in the middle of the road.

'What the fuck! Get out of the way!' the neighbours shouted.

At the trial he said he didn't see her until it happened, until he did it.

The eyewitnesses said different. It was deliberate. He just drove on until, *Wham!*

He heard the bump all right. Then he sped off. His solicitor said he was too frightened to stop. The prosecutor said that having committed his crime he did what one would expect a murderer to do. He fled the scene.

His missus landed forty feet away in the front garden of the neighbour two doors down from hers.

An ambulance came. The paramedics pronounced the girlfriend dead.

He was in a shebeen by this point. He drank all night.

The next morning he was asleep in the driver's seat of his car when two burly peelers approached and rapped on the glass.

He woke and wound the window down.

'Don't hit me,' he said. His speech was slurred. He was still very drunk.

'What are you talking about?' said the cop.

'I know, I'm a silly cunt but I'm going to kill myself, I've decided,' he said.

'Drunken Wifebeater Murders West Belfast Mother in Car Carnage Horror' was the headline in the *Sunday Muck* the following weekend. The story below the genius headline was sanitised so readers wouldn't be put off their breakfasts. It gave an account of McDowell's arrest and what he said: 'I know, I'm a silly c*** but I'm going to kill myself, I've decided.' The entire population of Loanend read the article and in a way both mysterious and typical, he ceased being Peter McDowell and became instead Silly Cunt, which was soon abbreviated to SC.

And now, standing near the boiler while clouds of steam gusted behind him, it was the man himself, SC, looking miserable.

The Escort screw left the class office and darted away down the back stairs to the circle below. Hayes came out of the class office and waved over to me.

'Chalky!' he said.

'Aye.'

'Get this man a bedding roll and what have you, and then put him in Cell 13, "F" wing.'

SC picked up his Loanend Suitcases and came forward. The top of his head was shiny. He'd shaved his hair off to try to look hard. It didn't work. His head looked like a peeled egg. The rest of him was all wrong too. His arms were too long, his feet were too big, and his shoulders were too narrow. He was like a puppet, light and flimsy. One slap and he'd crumple. I couldn't see his eyes because he wouldn't look back at Hayes or me. He kept looking round the circle. The poor sod was bewildered. That was normal because he'd just been sentenced. I reckoned he was scared as well in case somebody took a pop at him because of what he'd done.

'Right,' said Hayes. 'Chalky here will sort you out. Get your bed made then come up to the class office for a chat.'

I decided to act as if I didn't know who he was or what he had done or that he'd been in prison before. Pretending to be stupid usually gets you further if you're after information.

We went to the store. I got a bedding roll and a Welcome Pack. We humped them back to Cell 13 and dumped them on the metal prison bed.

'Pillow at the window end,' I said and pointed at the window with its three thick concrete bars, 'so the Night screw can see your head when he looks in at night. He's got to see you breathing.'

I waved at the Welcome Pack with its rough towel and cheap unbranded toiletries and plate and bowl and mug and cutlery all made of heavy green plastic.

'Whatever you do, don't lose the knife,' I said. 'It's the first thing the search team check.'

Cons had been known to melt the blade and embed a nail or screw or razor blade to make a shiv.

'I know,' he said.

'Oh really,' I said. 'How come?'

'The orderly on the remand wing told me the exact same thing when I come on there.'

'Oh right,' I said. 'So you've been here a while then?'

'Two years.'

'Oh, right. I was just wondering because I haven't seen you about.'

'I just kept my head down and got on with my whack,' he said.

'A stoic.'

'Yeah, whatever that is.'

'I'm Chalky.'

'Pete,' he murmured. He didn't mention his nickname.

I went back to my laundry duties. I passed Cell 13 later on and glanced up at the cell card in the little holder above the door. Hayes had filled it in and put it up. I knew his writing. Beside 'Tariff' was written '25 years'.

Jesus Christ, SC had to do a quarter century in here. But then those bleary drunken seconds when he'd been driving towards his victim were all premeditation time and the more premeditation time the longer you got when it came to murder.

Over the next few weeks, SC went to the furniture workshop every day to make cupboards and tables and shit for the cells as well as picnic tables and gazebos for the jail to sell. He stayed in his cell in the evenings. I'd say hello if I met him on the stairs or passed him on the wing but that was the height of it. I wasn't interested. He just wasn't interesting. So I'd hardly anything to do with him. He was a ghost in my life. He didn't come near me either. He didn't go near anybody really. He was quiet and probably lonely and I'm sure he felt pretty crap all of the time.

The weather was rotten and Loanend was even more cold and grey and miserable than usual. The whole jail was subdued and depressed. Hayes came to my door at a quarter to eight one evening.

'Lock-up in ten,' he said.

I got my Thermos and went to fill it with hot water from the boiler. When I was done and I turned to go there was SC right behind me, waiting his turn. He was staring at the floor.

'Well?' I asked cheerfully.

SC lifted his face. He looked like shit. He nodded and sighed. 'I'm grand,' he said and stepped forward to the tap.

Lock-up followed. I was vaguely aware that Gary was on again. I heard him limping by on his rounds. I went to bed and fell asleep. I slept through the hourly checks like usual but then I woke up. At first, when I opened my eyes, I couldn't work out why I'd woken up. I didn't usually. Then pretty quick I realised there was something going on out on the wing. I could hear heavy footsteps and screws talking. Their voices were quiet but they sounded anxious, very anxious.

I slipped out of bed and went to my cell door. The flap that covered the Judas slit was up. Screws will often leave the flaps up at night even though they're not meant to so it's quicker when they do their hourly check to make sure everybody's alive. This must have been Gary's doing.

I peered out but could only see across the landing. The voices were from further up the wing. Time passed. I heard a couple of other cons moving about in their cells. They'd been woken up and drawn to their cell doors like me. I heard a few wee coughs and the metallic click of a lighter as someone lit a fag. Then the schizophrenic in a top cell near the circle banged on his door and shouted, 'What the fuck's going on?'

That woke the whole wing up and pretty soon everybody was out of bed and shouting.

'What the fuck's happening?' shouted one.

'The fuckers are down in SC's cell,' said a second who could see.

'What the fuck are they doing? What are they at?'

'How the fuck would I know?'

Unable to answer our own questions, someone began to shout at the screws.

'Oi, you black bastards, what the fuck are yous doing to SC?'

'Shut the fuck up.' This was a screw. He beat the handle of his nightstick on somebody's door.

'You won't fucking shut me up that easy.' That sounded like Ciaran to me. He liked to pretend he was a Republican. Actually he was just a border fuel smuggler.

'Listen,' the screw shouted back, 'if you don't fucking shut it, I'm coming in to kick seven shades of shite out of you.'

Every con on the landing started to jeer and bang on his cell door. If the screws took on one con then they took on every con. The screw responded by beating his baton on a couple of doors though amazingly he didn't snap the flaps down to stop us looking like they usually do in this situation. He must have been in a panic. The racket we made was unbelievable. This went on for a wee while and then everybody got tired and hoarse and it stopped. When it was quiet again I could hear some sort of commotion in Cell 13. It was impossible to work out what it was but it definitely didn't seem right. Then I heard voices on the wing and footsteps. They were leaving.

I looked through the slit. A procession passed. First, I saw Gary and then a Medical Officer with a stethoscope around his neck and a bag slung over his shoulder with a big red cross on its flap. Four members of the riot squad in brown boiler suits followed next. They carried a stretcher. SC was on it. He flashed past and I didn't get a proper look at him but I got enough to know he'd done himself in. After the stretcher came four more Riot screws. They carried two shields each. A Night Duty SO and a Night Governor brought up the rear. The SO carried a board with every key to every lock in Block 3 hanging from a numbered hook and the Governor was a wee worried-looking man in a suit.

After the stretcher party passed, I imagined their journey up to the circle and along 'E' wing and down the main stairs and across the big downstairs Recreation Hall and through the grille to the downstairs circle and out the front door and across the squares and on to the prison hospital where an ambulance must be waiting. I felt sick.

Hayes unlocked me the next morning. His face was different to the one he usually had in the morning. He didn't say anything either which was also not like him. He put his finger to his lips. I nodded to show I understood. No questions. No talking. Yeah, I got it.

I shaved and dressed and went up to the class office. Murray was at the desk. Tank and Big Ben sat in the easy chairs. Hayes was at the counter. There was an atmosphere. There is always an atmosphere when a man tops himself on your wing. Suicide leaves you with this horrible fucking nagging feeling. You might have said something or done something to prevent it, maybe. And you can't stop yourself thinking this even if you weren't friends with the man who killed himself or didn't even like him. You feel guilty, you feel at fault. End of. Even the screws have these feelings.

I got cooking and the screws talked. They spoke in code but I got the story – what they had of it anyway.

Gary did his usual hourly cell checks – midnight, 1 a.m., 2 a.m., 3 a.m. After that one, knowing there was an hour before Gary's next check, SC tied a strip of sheet to the smoke extractor grille that had a noose at the other end. He put the noose around his neck and sat down. You haven't the drop in a cell when you hang yourself so that's what you do – you sit down to die and you stay sitting till you're dead. I've been told hanging yourself is just like having a shit, which makes it sound casual and like it's no big deal but that's bollocks. I can't imagine having to sit through your own death. Nor can I can imagine how much willpower and how much despair it takes to keep sitting, to keep the strain on, to keep the noose tightening around your throat, cutting the air until you die, until you're dead.

Every cell in the jail has an emergency button beside the light switch in a wee panel under the smoke extractor grille. SC hit his. He might've changed his mind or hit it by accident when he was thrashing around. It was a mystery but he hit it all right and that set off the emergency light above the cell door outside and a second light in the class office.

Gary saw the light, walked down and looked through the slit. He didn't see SC in the bed. He might have seen his feet down at the side of the door under the smoke extractor. He thumped the door and called SC's name. He got no reply. He hurried back as fast as he could to the class office and called Control. They brought the keys over. Cell 13 was unlocked but it was too late. SC was gone.

The cooking done, I set out four plates and dished up.

'I know I shouldn't be,' said Murray, 'but I'm fucking famished.'

The story of SC's life and death was splashed all over the *Sunday Muck* the following weekend. They quoted several unnamed sources from his old estate who said they were glad he was dead and the world was a better place without him. The hacks wouldn't have reported the story any other way of course. They love con suicides. They reckon if you don't have capital punishment it's the next best thing.

By the following Sunday SC was forgotten and he would have stayed forgotten only some suit decided to look at the tapes recorded on the night of his death by the cameras on 'F' wing.

The tapes made interesting viewing. The one from the class office camera showed that even though our Gary was meant to be awake all night he'd a lilo under Murray's desk that he slept on between his hourly rounds. He'd a wee alarm clock to wake him up. When the emergency light started to flash after SC pressed the bell Gary didn't see because he was asleep and he didn't see it till his alarm clock went off and woke him. The wing camera then showed him walking down to Cell 13 and looking through the Judas slit and then banging on the door and shouting in. Then boy did he move even with his limp. He dashed back to the class office to ring Control with an awkward lopsided shuffling gait as if he was drunk.

The other tape from the camera recording the screw over in the Control Room told a similar story. The Control screw's job was to watch all the Night screws and see they were all awake. So he should have seen that Gary was sleeping between rounds only he didn't because he was asleep as well. It was only when Gary rang him on the phone that he woke up. And because everyone was sleeping it was over an hour between when SC's cell bell went and when Cell 13 was unlocked and sometime during that time, SC died.

The tapes were leaked and a local TV company used them for a current affairs programme, *Sleeping on the Job: Death in Custody*. The night it went out every con in Loanend tuned in and the next day Gary and the Control screw were suspended pending further investigations. And the morning after, when I cooked their breakfasts, the screws talked about nothing else.

'It's a fuck-up all right,' said Murray.

'It's worse. It's a clusterfuck,' said Tank.

'Hang on,' said Hayes, 'instead of just sounding off, why don't you think about this problem rationally?'

'Go on, Mr Hayes,' said Murray. 'What are you trying to say?'

'Obviously, sleeping on the job is wrong.'

'What are you on about?' asked Big Ben. 'Many's the time I've seen you taking a crafty forty winks on our easy chairs. Aren't I right, Tank?'

'Yes, you are, Big Ben. That Hayes is a devil for sleeping on the job, so he is.'

'I am going to overlook that remark, you fat fuckers,' said Hayes.

'Ref, ref, Mr Murray, sir, he called us fat,' said Tank.

'Quit slabbering,' said Murray, 'and let Mr Hayes have his say. And pay attention. You might learn something.'

'The Night screw,' said Hayes, 'he's going to lose his job, pension, everything, as will the poor cunt in Control.'

'Oh he's got an issue,' said Big Ben, 'give him a tissue.'

'But even if they'd both been awake, SC would still be dead,' said Hayes carefully. 'It takes too long to get unlocked at night. We all know that.'

'And your point?' said Murray quietly.

'Our staff are being punished for something they wouldn't have been able to stop. It's the way we organise nights that's wrong, and that's what we should change rather than suspending those two.'

Murray sighed.

'I don't know,' said Murray. 'They should have been awake. They weren't. They pay the price.' He looked across at me. 'Oi, Chalky.'

'Aye,' I said.

'I want my bacon black, the pudding charred, the mushrooms shrivelled, the beans dried out, the eggs like rubber, the toast burnt and the tea cold. Do you think you can manage that?'

'I don't know.'

'Well you did yesterday,' said Murray.

The other three laughed. The bacon spluttered and the beans bubbled.

'You know,' said Big Ben, 'Night screws get paid shit. And you know what they say? You pay money, you get brains, or in my case, brains and looks, but you pay peanuts, you get monkeys. Isn't that right, Chalky?'

'Aye,' I said.

'And you're our monkey, right?'

I said nothing.

'Chalky, you can spit in Big Ben's brekkie if you like,' said Tank.

'I'll spit in yours, Tank,' said Big Ben.

Tank and Big Ben wrestled with one another on the easy chairs and laughed. Murray opened the *Daily Mail*. Hayes blew his nose.

Engine

'One on,' the Escort screw shouted. 'New boy,' he added.

He was wiry and brown. He carried two Loanend Suitcases with his name and prison number scrawled on the outside in felt tip. He'd just been sentenced but he didn't look stunned like men often do at this time. He looked calm and thoughtful. He was obviously not your run-of-the-mill con.

Hayes sauntered out of the class office and took the paperwork from the Escort screw and glanced at it.

'Right,' Hayes said, as if to say, 'Yes, we've been expecting him.'

The Escort screw left.

'Chalky,' said Hayes.

I was polishing the hot water urns on the other side of the circle.

'Aye.' I stepped across.

'Chalky's our orderly,' Hayes explained to the new prisoner. 'He's got your cell ready.'

The prisoner bowed solemnly. 'Thank you, sir,' he said. His voice was incredible. It was an actor's in an old black and white film. Nobody talked like that anymore, at least nobody I knew.

I brought him to the store and issued him with a bedroll and a Welcome Pack and led him to Cell 3 on 'F' wing. It smelt of piss and shite even though I'd given the toilet a good scrub. A pin board hung on the wall over the iron prison bed. There were nasty bits of graffiti scribbled in biro in the corners and smears of old toothpaste that had been used as glue to hold pictures up. The cell was small, cheerless and depressing.

'What do they call you?' I asked.

In his posh English accent, he said he was Sri Lankan so he had a Sri Lankan name but because he was a ship's engineer by trade his jail name, which he got while waiting for sentencing, was Engine. Obviously.

I set his bedroll and Welcome Pack on the mattress and he dropped his Loanend Suitcases on the floor and we shook hands. 'Chalky,' I said, 'from Chalkman.'

'Ah, chalk,' he said. 'What you write with on a blackboard?'

'Exactly.'

I offered him a roll-up. He accepted. We sat on the bed with the metal bin at our feet as an ashtray and we smoked and talked. He wasn't like anybody else I'd ever known in jail. He wasn't guarded and he didn't talk tough as if he had to prove he was a hard man. He seemed normal and friendly and I decided it was safe to ask him what I usually wouldn't think of asking a con.

'What happened to you? What are you in for?'

Engine shrugged. 'I have a partner,' he said. Then he shook his head. 'No, correction, I had a partner. Irish girl, Mary. We lived together in Belfast when I was not at sea. We had a daughter. Eleven years old now. We were not married, Mary and I. This was a mistake, not to marry.

'One day last year, Mary said the relationship was over and she asked me to leave the house. I got a knife and went to cut myself. I wanted to die. She tried to stop me. We fought. I pushed her away. I slashed her. She grabbed our daughter and the two of them ran out of the house. I cut my wrists.'

He raised a shirt cuff and showed me his left wrist. I saw a line of bumpy stitch marks.

'Ten minutes after I did this, the police came,' he said. He pulled his cuff down. 'I was arrested and charged with attempted murder. I was found guilty yesterday. I got ten years. My solicitor does not think an appeal is worth it. He said I should just do my time and then go home to Sri Lanka when I am finished. I am going to be deported anyway.'

'And what about your daughter?'

Engine shook his head. 'I have not seen her since I was arrested and I doubt I will ever see her again.'

He explained that after his arrest, Mary got a non-molestation order on the advice of the police. He was now prohibited from phoning or writing or approaching either Mary or his daughter in any way. If they'd been married it might have been different but they weren't so that was that. He was cut off from his daughter forever.

The people in Sentence Planning sent Engine to the metal workshop because he was an engineer. He was put to work making pokers and fireguards and ornamental gates. Engine left the wing at eight and came back at five smelling of engine oil and Swarfega five days a week. He mostly stayed in his cell at the weekends, meditating and saying his Buddhist prayers and doing yoga. He occasionally went to association in the big Recreation Hall downstairs and played table tennis or chess. Unlike a lot of the other cons, he was always friendly and would speak to anybody. As far as the other cons were concerned, he was just a poor wee foreigner who'd been screwed over by a woman and was forbidden to see his daughter, which hurt. A lot of them were in the same boat.

One evening I looked out of my cell window and I spotted Engine down in the yard walking round in circles with our Red Ken and Tiny.

Later that same evening, just before lock-up when I stood the best chance of nabbing him alone, I went to Engine's cell and put my head around his door and asked, 'Can I come in?'

'Yes, come in, Chalky,' said Engine. 'You want to convert to Buddhism?'

This was one of his jokes. He thought if everybody in Northern Ireland became Buddhist we'd stop being bigots.

He patted the bed. I sat.

'Those two ballsacks,' I said, 'who were walking with you in the yard earlier . . .'

'Yes.'

'Don't buy any drugs off them.'

'Why would I?' asked Engine. 'I would not do any of that. You know I would not. I don't take drugs.'

'And don't have anything to do with them, either,' I said. 'Don't hang about with them, don't associate with them, don't give them the time of day.'

'You are saying I must not to talk to them?'

'Aye,' I said. 'No contact, ever. Pretend they don't exist.'

'Why?'

'They're bad.'

'But I am not like other prisoners,' said Engine, 'who will not speak to this man because he is a sex offender, and that one because he is a tout. I talk to everyone, anyone. That is my way.'

'Engine,' I said, 'talk to anybody else, just not to them.'

'Your concern is touching,' he said, 'but you know me. I talk to everyone. I can't change that.'

Red Ken and Tiny hung out with Engine in the yard and in his cell over the next few weeks. There was something coming. I felt it.

And it came one Saturday evening. I was on my bed thinking about an old girlfriend and what she looked like with her kit off, when I heard screaming and jeering coming from the big Recreation Hall downstairs. The alarm bell for the Block went off and everybody was driven back to their cells and locked. That is SOP when the alarm in a Block goes. Everyone gets locked. But the rest of the prison carries on. It's only when the klaxon goes that you get a full lock-down of all of Loanend.

Garrett, a housebreaker, was in the cell directly below. I knew he always went to association in the Recreation Hall. He liked talking shit about committing the perfect crime with other men who liked talking the same shit. He'd tell me what had happened. I opened my window.

'Garrett,' I shouted between the bars. 'Go to your window.'

'Yeah, Chalky,' he shouted up. 'What is it?'

'What's happening, man? What was going on in the Rec Room just now?'

'Red Ken and Tiny,' Garrett shouted back, 'they fucked over some eejit over. Fuck, they did some number on him. I'd never seen him before so I don't know who he is, but they said he owed them money and he'd touted and they gave him a terrible battering. They'd knuckledusters.'

'What?' I asked.

'Knuckledusters,' he said again.

'Where did they come from?'

93

'Fucked if I know,' Garrett shouted back.

Half an hour later I heard the wail of a siren in the distance. It came from the direction of the prison hospital. The poor fucker who got the beating was over there by now and this was the ambulance come to cart him away.

I heard the siren for the second time a bit later as the ambulance drove off and then a wee while after that I heard the heavy tread of Riot screws as they tramped onto our wing. It is also SOP after any violence to swamp the block where the incident kicked off and strip-search all the prisoners and search their cells and turn the whole place upside down and teach us all a lesson we won't fucking forget.

I lay still and waited, expecting to hear keys turning and Riot screws telling prisoners they were to be strip-searched and to get their clothes off and prisoners shouting back but instead what I heard was the Riot screws just marching straight to Engine's cell and stopping. I heard his door being unlocked. Then there was a lot of banging as the Riot screws searched his cell and then I heard them leaving, taking Engine with them. As they passed up the wing I thought I could hear him sobbing. I assumed they were taking him to the Punishment Block.

Over the week that followed, I found out what happened by eavesdropping on the screws' talk and reading their log-book on the sly.

Red and Tiny had discovered Engine's story and then they found out where his ex and his daughter lived. That hadn't been hard with their contacts in a wee place like Belfast. Once they had they'd gone to Engine and made him an offer. They'd get any letters he wrote delivered to his daughter via the mother of his daughter's best friend and his ex-partner Mary would never find out. They guaranteed that. All Engine had to do in return was to make them knuckledusters in the prison workshop. Engine agreed as Red Ken and Tiny knew he would. His letters were smuggled out and he got to work. It wasn't easy. First he had to steal the metal. Then he had to make them when the Workshop screw wasn't watching. Knuckledusters were also tricky things to make. It took him a couple of tries before he got them right. Rather than dumping these first ones, Engine held onto them. That was stupid. He hid them in his cell. That was even stupider. And he told the Evil Twins what he'd done when he delivered the finished ones. That was the stupidest thing of all.

Red Ken and Tiny's victim was a wee twenty-one-year-old called Dessie McLaughlin. They broke his cheekbones, his nose, a fair few of his fingers, a couple of ribs, and knocked out half his teeth. They should have had the book thrown at them for that but they knew exactly how to work the system. After the attack, Red Ken and Tiny told the screws that Engine had made their knuckledusters in the metal workshop and to search his cell. The Riot screws did this. They found Engine's prototypes. Engine went to adjudication. He got a year's cellular confinement in the Punishment Block. Red Ken and Tiny only got three months because they'd cooperated even though they'd half-killed poor wee Dessie McLaughlin. They didn't even have to do their time in the Punishment Block but were allowed to stay on the wing.

Time passed. After he'd finished his sentence in the Punishment Block the jail didn't send Engine back to Block 3. They couldn't. Red Ken and Tiny were still on 'E' wing. Engine got sent somewhere else and I lost sight of him until one day when I was taking stuff to recycling I saw him standing outside the laundry. He wore a Walker's Pass: a red plastic ID that hangs on a lanyard around a man's neck that allows him to move about without an Escort screw. Engine was waiting to go into the laundry.

'Hello, Engine,' I said.

When Engine first came to jail, he never hid his face and he always met your gaze. Now he wore a baseball cap. I'd never seen him wear one before. He'd the cap pulled down and his eyes were in shadow.

'Chalky,' he said.

'You working in the laundry now?'

'Yeah, I'm in the fucking laundry,' he said, 'worse fucking luck.'

I'd never heard him swear before and I saw he saw how surprised I was.

'Yeah,' he said shrugging his shoulders.

I knew he was going to swear again, just to make sure I'd heard him right the first time.

'I'm in the laundry, with the fucking roots,' he said. 'And if I get the chance, I'm going to throw one of them fuckers inside the big washing machine and put it on a fast spin and kill the cunt.'

'That's not very Buddhist,' I said. 'What happened to you?'

'What happened?' asked Engine. 'You mean I wasn't like this when you knew me?'

'No, you were not,' I said.

'Well,' he said, 'I just spent a year in the Punishment Block and it was fucking horrible.'

'It's supposed to be,' I said.

The cells in the Punishment Block are smaller than the normal cells and the regime is much harsher and the Riot screws who run the place are headers.

'When I arrived the screws there told me they were going to fuck me over,' he said. 'They were going to put me where blackface wife-beating scummy bastards like me belonged – a hole in a bog – and all the prisoners in the block would be right behind them, cheering them on. I thought, what will I do? How will I survive?

'There was a man in the Punishment Block who'd killed a pregnant woman. She was driving when he stopped her car. He wanted it. She wouldn't give it. So he bashed her skull in with a crowbar. The baby died with her. He was a Rule 23 man. He was kept in his cell all the time for his own protection and only allowed out when everybody else was locked. The other men hated him and I knew if I didn't do something I was going to be hated just the same as him.

'I started slagging him like the other prisoners did, shouting at his window from the yard, banging on his door, making threats. The screws saw, the other guys saw, and you know what? Once they'd seen me slabbering and threatening like this they changed their opinion of me. Instead of being the scummy wife-beating black bastard they all decided I was all right. I was just like them. And once that happened I was sort of accepted, and once I was accepted I knew I was going to get through.'

'What are you telling me, exactly?' I asked. I thought I knew but I wanted to be sure.

He took his cap off. He looked at me. His face was not the face I remembered. It had changed. It had hardened. It had closed.

'Surely, you of all people must understand?' he said. 'You put on a mask and you keep it on and then what happens? After a while your skin and the inside of the mask grow together. They become one. And once that happens, you can't take the mask off again, not without pulling your face away with it and obviously you can't do that. So you are stuck, with the mask. It is now your face. You follow?'

I nodded.

'So, that's the story of Engine. He has grown into his mask and now he can't get it off.'

Sweet Gene

Hayes unlocked my cell just after two.

'Is the storeroom open?' I asked.

'Why,' said Hayes, 'are you there this afternoon, Chalky?'

'No, of course not,' I said. 'I'm popping into Belfast for a sauna. My taxi's on the way. Of course I am.'

Hayes smiled as he moved away to open the next cell along.

I went out my door and up the wing. All round me, cons were rushing off to trades or Education. The two o'clock unlock felt more like life outside than inside prison and that's why it's my favourite time of the day in jail.

The storeroom door was propped open with a plastic container of disinfectant. I turned on the light. It's a windowless room fitted out with metal shelves stacked with all the bedding and plastic eating utensils and toiletries a con needs in jail. One of my many jobs is to make up the Welcome Packs for the whole jail. I make thirty or forty a week. I can do one in about three minutes.

This is what I do:

First, with a lot of folding and creasing and pressing – Hayes calls it origami for cons – I transform a flat cardboard sheet into a box. It's like a pizza box only deeper. Next, no checklist required, I have it off by heart, I fill the box with cakes of soap and a shaving stick and a pack of disposable razors and a toothbrush and toothpaste and writing paper and envelopes and two Biros, one black and one red, and various printed materials including a Visitor's Order and a Tuck Shop form and a 43DF complaint form and the *Handbook of Prison Rules & Regulations* and the Kinlough Centre's booklet *Everything You Always Wanted to Know About HIV & AIDS, Alcohol & Drugs but Were Afraid to Ask* and a leaflet on the Listener Scheme. Job done, I fold down the lid stamped 'Her Majesty's Prison Loanend, Welcome Pack' and press the fasteners home. I was just starting to make up the second box when I heard a low wolf whistle behind me followed by, 'Look at those tits. I'd like a wee taste of her.'

I guessed whose harsh Belfast voice I was hearing and turned and saw I was right. We call him Torvill because his real name's Dean. He's an armed robber doing ten years. He usually wears a Man United strip and joggers but this afternoon he was in a Ben Sherman shirt and ironed jeans and dazzling white trainers fresh from their box.

'Visit?' I asked.

'Yeah, Sandra, my sister,' said Torvill, 'and she's bringing my daughters, since the wife won't do it.'

His wife now lived with the detective who'd arrested him. This was awkward for Torvill but hilarious for us.

'I'll be late back,' said Torvill. 'Will you keep my tea?'

'No sweat,' I said.

I did a fair few more packs and put on laundry. I got the steel dixies with the tea from downstairs at about half-three. I began serving at a quarter to four and by ten-past all the lads were fed. I was wiping the servery when Torvill appeared.

'Since you ask, Chalky, and thank you for your interest by the way, I'd a brilliant visit,' he said, 'and now I'm starving.'

'There you go.' I nodded at a styrofoam box.

'What is it?' he asked and began to undo the lid.

'Oh they done us proud tonight,' I said. 'Gammon steak. Pulled out all the stops.'

The lid lifted to reveal a slice of ham, dark brown and watery, a pineapple ring that was brown around the edges, a solid slab of grey mash and a tangle of onions that looked like bits of burnt, greasy wood. Torvill groaned and closed the lid.

'I've got some news for you,' he said. 'Your mate, Sweet Gene, he's back.'

'Hang on,' I said, 'he's not my mate. He's just someone I know.'

Eugene McKearney was a druggie. We'd been doubled up in a cell on Remand when he was in for possession and supplying and shoplifting charges. Sweet took any drug he could get his mucky wee hands on and that meant the search team turned us over nearly every other day. He whinged a lot about nobody ever helping him to get clean and though he was pleasant and shared his gear it was a relief when he got sentenced and moved on and I was on my own again in the cell. Torvill had been on the same wing at the time and that was how he knew I'd doubled up with Sweet Gene for a while.

'So,' said Torvill, 'he's not your mate, he's just your jail buddy. You know he's going to be broken hearted when he hears that, and trust me, he will, because he's coming back. You wanna hear the story? It's a cracker.'

'Do I have a choice?' I said.

'Nah.'

'Don't let me stop you then.'

'Earlier on today,' said Torvill, 'the sister, Sandra, and my girls are waiting at the wee turnstile at the front to come into the jail to see me when your mate, old Sweet, bowls up at the main gate, which is right beside the visitors' gate. The Gate screw recognises Sweet and thinks he's come up to visit somebody, so he tells Sweet to get in the queue behind Sandra. But Sweet Gene says, "I haven't come up to visit no cunt. See, I'm out on licence at the minute, but I just can't cope anymore. I'm back on the old drink and the old drugs and I'm robbing like nobody's business. Everything's away to fuck, so I've decided to revoke my own licence and turn myself in. I want back in the jail. Now. Right. Fucking. *Now*."

'Okay, all this is going on in front of all the visitors, including our Sandra and the girls. So, the old Gate screw goes, "Sweet, you can't just come in, not like this. You gotta go back to your probation officer and tell him and he'll decide whether to revoke your licence and send you back because that's what he's fucking paid to do, along with scratching his arse all day."

'But dear me, Sweet's having none of it. He starts screaming and shouting and kicking away at the gate like a madman, so the Gate screw gets on the phone and the cops turn up in a couple of minutes flat and they cuff Sweet and cart him away. He must be the first man in history ever arrested for trying to break back into jail instead of out of it. Anyway, rest assured, he'll be back with us any minute now. And you never know, Chalky. If you're lucky, you might get to double up with him again. Won't that be great? Remember all that fun yous had on remand? It'll be like Christmas.'

I shook my head.

'It wasn't fun and orderlies don't double-up. It's one of the perks of this shitty job,' I said. 'But I could put in a word for you, Torvill. Old Sweet'd make a great cellmate for you.'

'You do that, and you will eat your cock, mate,' said Torvill.

He took the styrofoam box with his dinner and swaggered away.

A few days passed. I was in the laundry room just off the circle. The dispenser drawer was gummed up with washing powder and I was cleaning it with an old toothbrush when I heard Hayes call, 'Chalky.'

I went out to the circle. There was Hayes and beside him with his head bent and his shoulders hunched stood Sweet Gene. He must have got what he wanted and got his licence revoked. Sweet had just the one Loanend Suitcase that was only about a quarter-full with his name and number on the side.

'I think you know Sweet Gene,' said Hayes.

That blabbermouth Torvill had told everybody on 'E' and 'F' wings not only about the scene at the gate but about our time together in the Remand Block. So Hayes knew I knew him.

'Hello, Sweet,' I said.

Sweet Gene lifted his head. He'd grey eyes and a long face with scars around the edges. These were the sites of boils he'd squeezed until they burst and scarred into pits. It's a common junkie thing. When they're coming down they can't help scratching at the pustules that come with using.

'Chalky,' Sweet replied. 'How's it hanging?'

'Well, apart from being in jail it's all hunky dory,' I said.

'Hunky dory,' he repeated slowly. His voice was whispery and papery and he didn't look right at me. There was nothing physically wrong that I could see but something about his eyes and the way he was standing said that inside his head things weren't at all right.

'Right, Sweet, in your own words, what happened?' said Hayes. 'You're among friends. Tell us the whole sad story. Why are you back?'

'Licence revocation.'

'Why was that?'

'I broke all the conditions.'

'And why did you do that?'

'I wasn't myself.'

'Right,' said Hayes.

'I was off my face.'

'Really,' said Hayes.

'I was using. And I did some street robberies.'

'Muggings you mean?' said Hayes.

'Aye,' said Sweet.

'Oh dear,' said Hayes. 'How many?'

'A fair few. But they were all stupid . . . I just grabbed handbags and legged it, that sort of thing. Didn't use no weapons or blades.'

'Well, that's a relief,' said Hayes.

Sweet said nothing.

'So, as well as a licence breach you've got new charges?' said Hayes.

'Aye,' said Sweet Gene sadly. 'But it's only Mickey Mouse stuff. The solicitor reckons I'll only get a few months.'

'Right,' said Hayes. 'So what are you looking at?'

'A year for the licence breach and another six months or so for the robberies . . .'

'So eighteen months and you're out,' said Hayes. 'That's not bad.'

'Aye, and then what?' said Sweet Gene. This was in a new tone. It was bitter and wheedling and bleak. 'Back out, into a hostel full of roots, no help, no money, so what's bound to happen next? I'll end up doing something stupid and I'll land back in this shithole again.'

Hayes sighed. He knew the truth when he heard it and this was the truth. Sweet had been in and out of jail his whole life and that wasn't likely to change.

'Sort Sweet out, will you?' asked Hayes. He told me Sweet's cell number. 'I'm going off to kill myself.'

I fetched a bedding roll and a towel and a Welcome Pack and then I led Sweet to Cell 4 and helped him make his bed.

'Any tobacco?' he asked when we were done.

'They take yours?'

'Aye.'

I wasn't surprised. I knew the bloody rule. New prisoners could only bring sealed pouches into Loanend. Open pouches were forbidden and got took off you in Reception and binned. This was to stop cons smuggling drugs in with their tobacco. It was a stupid rule because any con who was really intent upon bringing drugs in just stuck them up his arse. Since most guys came to Loanend with open pouches they lost their tobacco when they came in and they had to spend their first few days scrounging until they got an order through from the Tuck Shop.

I put a tuft of Golden Virginia and half a dozen Rizlas on Sweet's table.

'The tobacco's a gift,' I said.

'Thank you,' he said.

He sounded much sadder than I remembered him being when we were doubled-up. I might have to watch out for him for a while, I thought. It would be a bore but there are worse fates.

'You're a real friend,' said Sweet. 'I won't forget it.'

He meant it now but as soon as he got a sniff of any drugs he'd forget everything he'd ever said and everything he'd ever promised, and all he'd think about would be getting loaded. He couldn't help himself. He was a user.

Sweet Gene stayed behind his door for the rest of the afternoon. He didn't take his tea at four and he didn't unlock for evening association at five-thirty. At seven-forty Hayes shouted, 'Ten minutes to lock-up.' I went and knocked on Sweet's cell door because he hadn't been out.

'Sweet,' I said, 'do you want the lend of a Thermos so you can make a cuppa later? I have a spare I can lend you.'

'No, mate,' said Sweet Gene flatly. 'I'm all right.'

'What about smokes? I can shove some more under the door.'

'I'm all right, really.'

'What have you been doing?' I asked.

He had a TV in his cell – Hayes had dropped a set down – but I couldn't hear it so I knew it wasn't on.

'I can get you a paper if you're looking for something to have a read of. Or a wee puzzle book if you like doing crosswords. I can rip it in half and stick it in under the door.' There was a stack of them in the screws' class office.

'I've been writing,' said Sweet Gene.

I was surprised. I'd never thought of him as a scribbler.

There was scuffing at my feet. I looked down and saw a torn slip of lined prison notepaper sliding out from under his cell door. I picked it up and read the handwritten scrawl:

I'VE HAD IT WITH MY LIFE AND MY FUCK UPS. I'VE FUCKING HAD IT. EUGENE MCKEARNEY, PRISON NO. 4563Y

I went to the class office with Sweet's wee note. Hayes was sitting at the counter reading a newspaper.

'Are you about to spoil my evening, Chalky?' he asked. 'Because if you are, I don't want to know. At eight when the Night screw comes on, I'm going home to spaghetti Bolognese, a bottle of Rioja and my box set of *Breaking Bad*.'

'I think you should read this,' I said.

Hayes took the sheet and read it. 'Oh fuck,' he said. He picked up the phone and looked at me as he put the receiver to his ear. 'Okay, you can go now.'

I went to my cell and closed my door over and then I smoked a roll-up at the window and looked up at the clouds.

One was like an exploding bag of soot and another looked like a lion's head. The screws were locking everybody for the night. There were doors slamming and locks turning everywhere. I heard my door swing open and I turned and saw Hayes at my door.

'Thanks for earlier,' he said. 'Sweet's going to the Safe Cell, once everyone's locked.'

'Is that the best idea? That place makes you crazier than you already are,' I said.

Hayes shrugged. 'Come on, you know we don't do best here. We do least worst.'

He locked my door. Out on the wing the lock-up was over and done with. It was quiet. I heard Hayes's soles squeaking on the linoleum as he padded off to Sweet Gene's cell. I thought about the Safe Cell at the top of the wing. It was the closest cell to the class office. It was originally Cell 1. Just a bog-standard cell but after SC's death it was decided a special cell was needed for self-harmers and suicides.

I knew it well. I'd cleaned it often enough. It's like the sickbay in a cheap sci-fi film. It's all white. There are no sharp corners for a con to put out his eye on and no toilet seat for a con to smash into slivers to cut himself with. All the furniture's bolted down and indestructible. The mattress and bedding are made of material that can't be torn into strips for a noose. It's the same textile that's used to make bullet-proof vests. Safe Cell prisoners also have to wear a special gown made of the same stuff. It's mauve and quilted and floor length and it ties at the back like a straitjacket. When you need the toilet you just lift the skirts and hey presto. Underwear's never worn. No underwear allowed in the Safe Cell. No trainers either. Only clogs. And if all this isn't bad enough, there's a camera in the Safe Cell with a permanent feed to the class office *and* the Control Room. You can't even wank in the Safe Cell without being seen. There's no privacy and the cons fucking hate it.

Down the wing I heard Hayes asking Sweet Gene to put on the special gown and Sweet Gene roaring back, 'I'm not wearing that fucking thing.' I heard Hayes slam the cell door and hurry to the class office.

About half an hour later I heard the Riot screws tramping onto the wing. The prisoners began shouting abuse as they always do when the Riot screws are about. Then I heard the screws in Cell 4. They were cutting Sweet Gene's clothes off with the special pair of scissors they've got for that while Sweet screamed with rage and shame. Then I heard them trussing him up in the dressing gown and dragging him down the wing and throwing him into the Safe Cell. Job done, they walked away banging cell doors as they passed with their baton ends and shouting at the cons, 'Excitement over! Settle boys, settle ... ' There was a bit more jeering but as soon as the Riot screws left everything quietened down pretty quickly.

The next day and the day after and the one after that, Sweet was kept under continuous observation in case he did something silly. He had no contact with any prisoners and we were forbidden to speak to him. According to staff, this psychic quarantine, as they called it, was good for the prisoner. It was torture if you asked me. If you aren't mad before you go in the Safe Cell you certainly will be by the time you get out.

I was in the Recreation Room on 'E' wing on the afternoon of the fourth day. There'd been barbering there all morning and the floor was covered with hair. All those wee hairs were a real bastard to sweep up. Hayes appeared.

'Chalky,' he said, 'follow me and bring your broom.'

We traipsed round to 'F' wing and passed the Safe Cell and arrived at Cell 4, Sweet's cell. Hayes unlocked the door. I looked in. The Riot screws had taken Sweet's cut-up clothes away though there were still threads and scraps on the floor.

'Okey doke,' said Hayes. 'First dig out some clothes for Sweet Gene and bring them down to the Safe Cell. Then come back, tidy up and run the broom over the floor.'

Hayes went away and I went in and leant my broom against the wall. I saw Sweet Gene's single Loanend Suitcase sitting in the rickety open wardrobe. He hadn't unpacked anything. Then I noticed something lying under the table. It was a sheet of prison notepaper with writing on it. The writing was Sweet's. I picked up the sheet:

MY LIFE BY EUGENE McKEARNEY 4563Y.
MY DA IS A FUCKING ALKY. HE NEVER LOVED US. HE JUST LOVES BOOZE. I WON'T FORGIVE HIM BUT I DON'T FORGET HIM AND IN MY PRAYERS I STILL PRAY FOR HIM EVEN IF HE IS AN ALKY CUNT. BUT I NEVER FUCKING WANT TO SEE HIM EVER AGAIN. HE CAN ROT AND DIE IN CORK.

MY MA IS A FUCKING JOKE. SHE DON'T CARE ABOUT PROMISED TINY AND RED I'D MEETAS KIDS AND SHE STILL DON'T. SHE WAS A FUCKING PISS HEAD AND SHE STILL IS, HER AND THE MUPPET SHE LIVES WITH.

WHEN I WAS SIX MY DA AND A LOAD OF MEN PUT A MATTRESS OVER HER HEAD AND MADE ME AND DOROTHY AND HELEN WATCH WHEN THEY DID IT. BAD AS ALL THAT WAS IT WAS WORSE WHEN THEY DONE IT TO ME. I WAS IN CARE AFTER THAT. CARE IS SHIT.

I COME OUT AT SIXTEEN. I'VE BEEN IN AND OUT OF EVERY FUCKING JAIL ON THIS FUCKING ISLAND EVER SINCE. MY LIFE WILL NEVER CHANGE AND I AM A CUNT.

I put the sheet on the table face down and opened Sweet's Loanend Suitcase and picked up some clothes and a pair of trainers and left.

I found Sweet in the Safe Cell standing by the window. He was staring out at the sky. Hayes stood behind Sweet and he was undoing the straps of the gown.

'I've told the PO you're settled, you're calm, and you won't hurt yourself,' said Hayes. 'So don't do anything silly. Just go back to your cell, do your whack, and when you're done, go away and don't fucking come back.'

I dropped Sweet Gene's clothes and trainers on the bed.

'I'll get things straightened up in Sweet's cell,' I said and left.

I saw Sweet at dinnertime when he came to the circle for his food. He was wearing a crucifix on a plastic chain.

'You all right?' I gave him an oily burger inside a thin bun with a portion of cold chips.

'I've been praying,' he said.

He hadn't gone mad. He'd found God instead, which often happens. I couldn't see it lasting.

The following week I noticed Sweet Gene and the Evil Twins nattering in the yard. It hadn't taken them long to find each other. The crucifix was gone when he came for his grub at dinnertime.

There was a full cell search on 'E' and 'F' wings the next day. It was a nightmare. We were all strip-searched and then the Riot screws turned the place upside down. They found diazepam and ecstasy in Sweet Gene's cell as well as antipsychotics and antidepressants belonging to a nervous sex offender. Sweet was carted away to the Punishment

Block and held overnight. He was adjudicated the next morning. It took about a minute. The Riot screws said what drugs they'd found and the adjudicating Governor handed out the sentence. Sweet got a fortnight in the Punishment Block. He did the first three days in a dry cell. There was no toilet and no window and no TV and no tobacco. He did the rest in a punishment cell. Here he had a toilet and a window and a TV and tobacco but no lighter. He could only get a light from a screw on request. Having to beg for lights was the worst part of it because the Riot screws' usual response was, 'Fuck off.'

When Sweet returned, he announced he was through with drugs and was just going to do his whack and get out. He sounded like a man trying to talk himself into following a course of action he didn't believe in. You didn't need to be a clairvoyant to know how this was going to go.

The next time the Riot screws searched Sweet's cell they found LSD and hash and a SIM card for a mobile phone and a blade. He said the blade wasn't his and he was holding it for somebody else but he owned up to the rest. He got twenty-one days in the Punishment Block. When he came back to the wing Sweet again swore he was going clean. A few days later more drugs were found in his cell. He got four weeks at his adjudication for that.

I lost track of Sweet Gene after that as he to-ed and fro-ed between his cell and the Punishment Block as well as making a short trip to an outside court for the muggings. He pleaded guilty and got a Determinate Custodial Sentence or DCS of six months' jail followed by three years on licence. The six months was to run consecutively to the twelve months he'd to serve for breaking his licence. That meant Sweet Gene had to do eighteen months altogether minus time spent on remand.

And then the day came when Sweet's eighteen months were finally up and his sentence was done. I saw him outside the class office with his Loanend Suitcase a few minutes before he was about to leave. I went over and shook his hand.

'Good luck,' I said. 'And try not to fuck up your licence like you did last time.' He'd have to serve whatever was left of the three years in jail if he did.

'I won't,' said Sweet.

Hayes strolled out of the office.

'Whatever you do, Eugene,' he said, 'please don't come back, do you understand, because I don't want to see you again, ever. Got that?'

'Aye,' said Sweet Gene, smiling.

'Right, your escort's downstairs. Off you go and good luck.'

Sweet vanished down the back stairs.

'I stopped smoking five years ago,' said Hayes, 'and every day I've had to deal with Eugene McKearney this last while, you know what, I've had this terrible urge to light up.'

A few months later, I was cleaning out the soap dispenser in the laundry room again.

'Chalky!' Hayes shouted.

I put my head round the door. I saw Sweet Gene with a Loanend Suitcase on the other side of the circle.

'Get what he needs from the store,' said Hayes, 'and meet us at Cell 5.'

Sweet was inside standing by the table and staring at the floor when I got to the cell door and Hayes was in the wing.

'Put it on the bed and step out of the cell,' said Hayes.

I set the Welcome Pack and the bedding roll on the bed and stepped out. Hayes swung the door shut behind me and turned the key.

'Fucked his licence, so he's back,' said Hayes. He jiggled the keys and went to put them in his pocket and then decided against it.

'What's it all about, Chalky?' asked Hayes. 'Well, since you ask, I'll tell you. A man comes in, does his time, leaves, messes up again, and comes back. That's it, day after month after year, that's it. That's it. That's all there is. And meantime, what about me? Well, I just get a little bit older, a little bit fatter and a little bit more stupid. Did you get that, McKearney?' he called back through the door.

No word came from the other side.

Hayes walked off, swinging his keys. After three steps, he stopped and turned.

'Chalky,' he called back to me.

'Aye.'

'I'm dying for a smoke, mate.'

I fished my tin from my pocket.

'I'll roll you a couple,' I said, 'and slide them under the door into the class office.'

'Good lad,' Hayes said.

'And me too,' Sweet murmured from the other side of the door. 'Don't forget about me.'

'How could I?' I said. 'That'd be impossible.'

The ABC Con

According to the prison shrink who did a report on me recently, I'm very selfish. I wouldn't disagree. I am. Only I'd add this: I'm selfish in a good way.

The time, Sunday afternoon, the place, 'E' and 'F' wings Recreation Room. A tabloid, the *Sunday Muck*, was going from prisoner to prisoner. It was full of lurid articles about criminals and their trials that we all read carefully of course, either because we knew the men, or because there was a chance they'd be joining us, or both.

One of the articles was about Seanie McDonagh, a traveller. It was his first offence so nobody knew him. According to the hack who'd written it, Seanie lived on a halting site with his mother on the edge of West Belfast. He was a drug dealer. He was up for possession and dealing. He was also up for rape. One of his buyers was a girl who couldn't pay so in lieu of a few pounds he screwed her. She was twelve though Seanie thought she was eighteen. Or so the article said he said. The judge wasn't impressed with Seanie's defence. Neither were my fellow cons that afternoon.

Show his face up here we'll show him, fucking raping paedo cunt, they muttered. I said nothing. They hadn't a mission. These guys were talking shit. Bloody blowhards.

A few days later, I was in the storeroom counting stuff.

'Chalky!' I heard Hayes bellow.

I stepped out of the storeroom and padded down the corridor, cells to the left and right of me. It was quiet. Everyone was either at work or locked.

I crossed the circle at the top and got to the class office door.

'Enter,' said Hayes from inside.

I went in. I found Hayes staring up at the whiteboard that lists the names and prison numbers and cell numbers of the cons on 'E' and 'F' wings.

'Can you get Cell 2 ready?' said Hayes. 'Bedding roll, Welcome Pack, you know the drill.'

'Yes.'

'Give it a brush out as well.'

'Certainly,' I said.

'Don't you want to know who the new arrival is? I bet you do, you nosey bastard.'

'No, I'm happy to wait,' I said.

Not true but I wasn't going to let him know that. In a jail the more you keep hidden, and the less anyone knows about you, the better.

'I admire your restraint.'

'Thank you, Mr Hayes.'

Through the office window I heard the sound of jeering, the ugly kind that puts you on edge. It came from the Punishment Block. Some poor fucker, probably a Rule 23 who was going to be kept in isolation for his own protection, was getting a roasting from the cons who weren't Rule 23s and were there for punishment.

'Our new guest's name is Seanie McDonagh,' said Hayes. 'He's a tinker, sorry, itinerant.'

He paused deliberately so I could admire his correction. I remembered the *Sunday Muck* article but didn't let on. That's the way. Say nothing. Show nothing. Nothing.

'I'll get the cell ready,' I said.

'You do that,' said Hayes.

Seanie was sentenced to ten years and arrived carrying two paper sacks full of his clothes. He was early twenties, short hair, wide forehead, big face, little mouth, sharp chin. His body was massive – big arms, huge thighs, plenty of thick muscle. From the size of him, and the way he stood, and the way he lifted his head and looked around, I knew he'd be lethal in a scrap. Oh yeah, he could really fight and that, plus the word, which had come in from other travellers in Loanend, that he wasn't to be touched, would keep him safe. My fellow prisoners who'd been talking so hard on Sunday in the Recreation Room mightn't be friendly to Seanie but no way would they take a pop at him now. Do that and they'd have to take on his whole tribe and they hadn't the balls for that. Of course they hadn't.

I issued Seanie with his bedding roll and his Welcome Pack and helped him make the bed and get the place generally ship shape and then, glancing round his cell, which frankly looked fucking dismal, there was absolutely nothing in it, I asked him how he planned to pass his first evening as a sentenced man. I knew he wouldn't get his TV for a couple of days on account of us being out of them, so this was an important question.

'Dunno,' he said.

'There's a shelf of paperbacks up on the circle. Jeffrey Archer, that sort of stuff. Take one.'

'I don't think I'd like that,' he said.

'The screws have puzzle books with crosswords, Sudoku, that sort of shite. I could get you one.'

'I don't think I'd like that,' he said.

He sounded flat, lonely, baffled and sad. Of course he did. He'd just moved into a pissy cell which smelt of spunk and toilet disinfectant. It was cold and cheerless and dreary and he was going to be in here for years with no one but himself for company. I know he'd only himself to blame but knowing that was no help to him. When a man starts a sentence, whether or not he accepts what he done and Seanie frankly didn't, it's just fucking depressing, and what you have to do, what you must do, is get busy, get occupied, immediately, otherwise the mood gets a grip on you and then you're fucked.

'So what are you going to do?' I asked.

'Dunno.'

'Look,' I heard myself saying, 'I've got this matchstick kit I got months ago from the Tuck Shop. It's for an Irish high cross or something. Some old Gaelic thing anyway. I opened it and that's as far as I got. Not for me, I realised. I don't have the patience. Why don't I get you it? You can have it.'

He looked at me. He wasn't sure. Was I trying to scam him?

'Don't worry, it's a gift, you won't owe me anything.'

He was still unsure.

'I'll fetch it. I'll leave it with you. You don't want it, give it back tomorrow. I can't say fairer. What do you say?'

He nodded. I fetched the box back to him. I took off the lid and laid out the plan which explained in pictures how to build the cross. I showed him how to use the match cutter and I checked the glue was still soft in the bottle. It was.

'You're ready to go,' I said. 'See how you get on. If you're not interested, give it back tomorrow.'

'You really don't want it?' he said and I said I really didn't want it and it looked to me like he believed what I said and he was happy with that and so was I. You see, I felt sorry for him, first night of a ten-year stretch, and I believed it might help the poor cunt pass the time.

Seanie had the kit assembled, sanded, varnished and painted within the week and at two foot high I have to say it was impressive. Then Hayes supplied Seanie with more matchsticks – Hayes did this out of pity – and he began making matchstick thingamajigs of his own design like a CD rack, a tobacco tin, and a box for playing cards, and as he got better he began to introduce patterns into his work. Matchstick knack-knacks are common in jail and lots of cons make them but Seanie's were a cut above the usual stuff: they were well-made, nicely finished, and even attractive.

Seanie got a job with the garden squad, doing the hanging baskets round the jail, mowing grass, putting up fences, that sort of thing, all manual, no paperwork, which suited him down to the ground he said, and he spent his evenings either watching the TV he eventually got or making his matchstick novelties. As jail lives go it wasn't too bad, but then of course Seanie had to go and fuck it up, didn't he? He just couldn't stop himself nicking things from other men, anything he could lay his hands on. He got away with it for while though everyone suspected he was at it and then one day he went into Bumper Boyle's cell on 'E' wing and lifted a pint of milk plus a bar of chocolate, and Boiler, as he was known – he'd glassed a man in a pub and taken his eye out and was doing eight – met Seanie coming out of his cell holding the milk and chocolate he'd nicked, and Boiler was so angry he hit Seanie a belt and then he raced round to Seanie's cell and smashed every single thing Seanie had made out of matchsticks before Seanie could get there to stop him, and everyone in the jail agreed, including those of Seanie's stripe, that this was fair. A prisoner is caught stealing from another prisoner, which is a heinous crime in our book, he gets what he deserves and he takes it.

A few hours after Boiler's wreck-up, I found Seanie in his cell with tears and snot running down his face and his bin at his feet filled with his smashed up matchstick whimsies and his Irish cross.

He was going to get Boiler, he told me, and he was going to kill him. This was not a good idea, I said. He might be lethal but so was Boiler. They'd just end up knocking lumps out of each other. A better idea, I argued, was to appear indifferent. 'Just act like you don't fucking care,' I said.

'How?'

'Get new matchstick kits from the Tuck Shop, start building. Make another Irish high cross, or an Irish caravan, or an Irish cottage – anything. That's the way to win. Show you don't care.'

After a long conversation he agreed.

'Where's your Tuck Shop form?' I said. 'Let's do it now.'

As I spoke I saw something on his face and I realised, of course, Seanie didn't read or write and I knew I'd known this all along only I hadn't let myself know I knew it until now, and the moment after I twigged the strangest, weirdest idea came into my head. Why did it come? I can't tell you. It was just one of those things you don't plan and you can't explain but that happen.

'Tell you what,' I said and I put my idea to him. He'd make me the alphabet, big and small letters, out of matchsticks, and each letter would be half a matchstick deep, and I'd pay him fifty grams of tobacco, plus I'd cover the cost of the materials. Seanie thought there was some scam involved and it took me a while to convince him. Then I got some paper and a letter stencil from the art teacher, Mrs Cartmill, drew the letters out for him and off he went. Three weeks later, bish, bash, bosh, he had it done, the alphabet, twice, big and small, and that was the moment, as I paid him his fifty grams, I put the next part of my plan into action.

'Why don't you sign up for the literacy class,' I said. 'Mrs Gregg's coming down the wing getting names. Why not put your name down?'

He looked doubtful and annoyed.

'What's that?' I pointed at 'Z'.

'Z,' he said.

'And that?'

'P.'

'And that?'

'M.'

'See, you're the ABC con. You know the alphabet already. You're half way there, but all the other guys in the class will know Jack shit. You'll be the star. Plus, have you seen Mrs Gregg?'

Seanie knew that I was making sense and when Mrs Gregg appeared at his cell door – blonde hair, big tits, perfume, she featured in the fantasies of all of us who knew her when we wanked – he said, 'Yes,' and she added his name to her list and beamed.

And that was that. Seanie started two days later and over time, as he put it, he got the word.

We became friends and then, now he was my mate and he felt he owed me one, I got him to steal to order from the gardens for me, among other things a big flathead screwdriver that our resident hooch maker needed so that he could open the electrics boxes on the wings because inside they were warm and the booze fermented in them beautifully and the hooch maker paid for the screwdriver with an enormous lump of blow that Seanie and me took a fortnight to smoke.

If the shrink got wind of any of this what would he say? Manipulative narcissist? Or a good, loyal friend?

Cell 13

'My sleep,' announced Ricky from the doorway of Cell 13.

'What about it?'

I was only a couple of feet away from him. I was using a big machine with felt pads to buff the linoleum of the corridor that ran between the cells on 'F' wing.

'Banjaxed!'

'Why's that?' I asked. 'Guilty conscience?'

Ricky had knocked a bloke unconscious in a club and then thrown him off the fire escape and into the car park forty feet below. It was a drugs dispute. He'd got life with a tariff of twenty years. I didn't like Ricky and I never had. He liked to make out he was a big shot when he wasn't. He was just a small-time dealer who lost the plot one night and acted like a dick.

'No, Chalky,' he said quietly, 'the reason I can't sleep is because it's haunted.'

I turned off the buffer and clicked the arm into its keeper.

'Mental,' I said. 'Tell us about it. I'm all ears.'

'Don't take the piss.'

'I wouldn't dream of it. Go on,' I said.

'Well,' he said, 'there's a presence in there at night. It's fucking killing me, I'm telling you.'

He indicated Cell 13 immediately behind with a backwards nod.

'And how do you explain it?' I asked.

He looked down at his feet and then at me. 'SC topped himself in there, didn't he? I'd say it's something to do with that.'

'But hang on,' I said. 'Nobody who was in Cell 13 after SC and before you moved in ever said anything about a presence. You're the first. How do you explain that?'

'Well, I'm sensitive and ah – my ma's a bit psychic.'

'Oh right,' I said, 'well that explains it then.'

'Look,' said Ricky, 'I don't care what you think, or whether you believe me or not, but I am telling you, hand on heart, not a word of a lie, it's in my cell, every night – a something, whatever it is, and it's doing my head in.'

'What does this presence look like?'

'You think I fucking look?' he said. 'Are you mad? I hide under my covers till morning unlock.'

I considered the situation. He really was in some state. Here was an opportunity, I realised, and one I should take advantage of. But I'd have to be quick – and decisive.

'Two fifty gram pouches of Golden Virginia and ten phone cards, and I'll swap cells with you,' I said. 'You can go into Cell 11 and I'll go into 13. Just square it with the screws.'

Ricky went down to the class office to ask. I was summoned five minutes later. I found him inside with Hayes.

'Chalky, you're agnostic, right,' said Hayes, 'so you don't do ghosts, do you?'

It's a funny thing but everybody automatically assumes only believers believe in ghosts while nonbelievers don't. If I said 'I don't do God but yes I believe in ghosts' then this cell swap wasn't going to fly but if I said, 'No, Mr Hayes, of course I don't,' or similar then it was.

'No,' I said. 'I don't do ghosts.'

'Ricky here,' said Hayes, 'isn't happy with his accommodation. Normally, we don't move inmates at their request, but, if the orderly asks that's different. I take it you're requesting a cell swap, Chalky?'

'Aye.'

'Say it then.'

'What?'

'I am requesting a cell swap.'

'I'm requesting a cell swap,' I said.

'Lovely,' said Hayes. 'Chalky, you are now in Cell 13, and Ricky, you are in Cell 11.'

We swapped our gear around. I got into bed at about eleven. I turned on the television. 4Music came on. I watched Beyoncé singing 'All the Single Ladies'. She was so close I could've reached out and touched the screen from where I lay. That wouldn't do me any good of course so

I decided to stop torturing myself and turn in instead. I muted the TV and turned it off and slipped the remote under my pillow. I muted it in case I accidentally turned it on in the middle of the night. I put the remote under my pillow because that was where I kept it safe from cell thieves just like every other con did. For some obscure reason cell thieves only stole remotes left out in plain view and never took ones stashed under pillows.

I went to sleep quickly with no qualms and no anxieties. I awoke a couple of hours later. There was a sound. It was watery and scratchy and it filled the small concrete box that was Cell 13. It wasn't a mechanical sound or an electrical sound. It was the sound of something living and I didn't like it one wee bit. My thighs trembled and my stomach curdled. I told myself that ghosts didn't exist. There's no such thing as ghosts. You're imaging things, I said to myself. It's only a stupid wee noise. Ghosts don't exist.

I raised my head. The cell light was off but the security lights outside shone through the bars. I saw the outlines of my table and the television and the cell door and the hand basin and the partition that screens the toilet so you can't be seen taking a shit when somebody looks in through the Judas slit. I needed to turn the light on but the switch at the door was too far away.

Then I'd a brainwave. I slipped the remote from under my pillow and pressed 'On' and jumped up. The television came on and by the light from the screen – it was a Michael

Jackson video for 'Beat It', picture only – I saw something slithering over the toilet rim. It was a rat. It must've swum in under the U-bend of the toilet. A big wet fucking rat.

'Christ!'

I wrenched the duvet up and threw it behind without thinking. I didn't want the rat climbing up the duvet from the floor and getting at my feet. The rat sprang off the toilet to the floor and ran under the table the TV sat on. It was dark under there and I couldn't see him but I could feel him. He'd a presence all right.

'Jesus!'

I managed to lean across to the control panel by the cell door without getting off my bed. I turned on the overhead light first and then I hit the cell alarm button. This activated the lights above my cell door and in the class office, where I hoped the Night screw was awake and alert and ready to spring into action. I thumped the cell door a couple of times for good measure.

'Jesus Christ!' I shouted. 'There's a rat in my cell!'

I retreated to the middle of my bed. The rat scurried along the narrow patch of linoleum at the side of my bed to the wardrobe in the corner directly across from my pillow. There was food from the prison Tuck Shop on the top shelf. I'd Hobnobs and Pot Noodles and teabags up there. So that was his game. The dirty wee fucker.

I reached over and grabbed a tin of sweetcorn and hurled it at him. I missed. It hit the plywood bottom of the wardrobe and rolled to the back. I lifted a tin of pears and flung it. It hit the floor. The sound it made was a dull sound like something heard through cotton wool. A hollow clump. The rat scampered back the way he'd come with his long pink tail swishing behind. He got himself into the corner by the door. That was as far as he could get from me in an eleven by seven-and-a-half foot cell. There were footfalls outside. The flap over the Judas slit lifted. The Night screw's nose and eyes were bathed in red light from the emergency light whirring above.

'What is it?' the Night screw shouted in.

'There's a rat in here.'

'What do you expect me to do about it?'

'Unlock the door.'

'And let it out onto the wing?'

'Well, you have to do something.'

Philly in the cell opposite mine but one was now awake.

'Get a dog, then unlock the cell,' he shouted. 'The dog will get it.'

'Oh, good plan,' said the Night screw. 'Middle of the night, yes, there's bound to be a dog somewhere.'

'No,' I said, 'forget about the dog. Just unlock the cell and let me out.'

'How am I supposed to do that?' asked the Night screw. 'The keys are in the Control Room.'

They didn't keep keys on the landings at night. How'd I forget about that?

'Well, ring and get them brought over,' I shouted.

'All right.' He sounded weary. 'I'll phone over to Control.'

He turned off the emergency light on the panel outside my cell. The red disappeared and now it was white light from the wing ceiling lights that I saw through my Judas slit. The Night screw went off. He'd forgotten to close my flap.

'Hey, Chalky,' shouted Philly, 'got any chocolate?'

'What?'

'Have you chocolate?'

'Aye.' I'd a Cadbury's Fruit & Nut up with the Hobnobs and the Pot Noodles.

'Rats love chocolate. Throw a bit onto the floor and wait till he comes – and he will, believe me – and then – wallop.'

'What do you mean "wallop"?'

I was watching the rat – he was very still and he was watching me back.

'Squash him.'

'With what?'

I watched the rat's tail. It snaked away along the floor. It moved and trembled slightly.

'Your TV.'

'My TV?'

'Yeah, drop your fucking TV on him.'

I didn't think. There was no time. I got straight to it.

I leaned over and unplugged the TV and lifted it onto my bed. The rat watched and his nose raised slightly into the air. I pulled my bar of Cadbury's Fruit & Nut from the wardrobe shelf and tore the wrapper open and broke off four squares and dropped them on the floor beside my bed. Then I lifted the TV in both hands and leaned out over the floor.

There was a pause. It felt like a very long one. My arms were starting to ache with the weight of the TV and my awkward position. Then the rat moved nonchalantly from the corner where he was to the chocolate and began to scrape with his large white teeth at a square. Then he stopped. My arms trembled with tiredness and fear. He was going to carry the chocolate back to the corner. I knew I'd never kill him there. It was now or never. I dropped the set. There was a crunchy sound of splintering plastic and breaking glass. There was another long pause. I waited. I listened. I heard wee tinkling sounds coming from inside the smashed TV while I waited. These were the sounds of broken components settling. I thought of a sunken ship coming to rest on the seabed floor. I heard no scratching. Nothing like that. There was no sign of the presence. I waited. I listened. No, nothing.

'Victory?' Philly shouted.

'I think so.'

'I'll push my bell.'

Through the Judas slit I saw the red light from Philly's cell door.

The Night screw returned.

'No need for the dog,' shouted Philly.

'Success?' the Night screw shouted in to me.

'Just get the key,' I said.

I sat down on my bed. I had no intention of lifting the TV to see what was underneath. That could wait. I pulled the duvet around me. Time passed. I waited. I heard footsteps again and then the sound of keys jingling outside the cell door. 'Took your time, didn't you?' Philly shouted from across the corridor. The key was inserted and the lock slid inwards and the door opened. I saw a Key screw and a Control screw and the Night screw out in the corridor. The Night screw had a brush handle.

'Evening,' said the Night screw. His tone was cheerful and slightly sarcastic. The other two behind stared in.

'Where is he?' asked the Control screw.

'Under the TV.'

'I don't like rats,' said the Key screw.

'Join the club,' I said. 'Free lifetime membership.'

I saw the Control screw get down on his knees outside the door and put his cheek to the linoleum and squint along the floor.

'I can't see anything,' said the Control screw.

The Night screw came into my cell. I stood up on the bed.

'Right, let's see if the little fucker has nine lives,' said the Night screw.

He prodded the TV with the end of the brush handle. More tinkling followed but no scratching.

'See anything?' he shouted back to the Control screw.

The Control screw was still down with his cheek to the floor squinting along the linoleum. 'Yes, the cunt's there all right,' he said.

'Is it alive?'

'I don't fucking know. He's not moving anyhow.'

'Right-oh, in for a penny, in for a pound,' said the Night screw.

The Night screw pushed at the TV with the brush handle until it toppled over onto its side with a crash that was abnormally loud in the silence of the early morning. I looked down at the dead animal. Its fur was wet and slick and the skin showing through the fur was pink and its tail was leathery and in its mouth, in its long sharp teeth, was a square of my chocolate.

'It's fucking enormous,' said the Night screw.

Out on the wing the Control screw got up from the floor and dusted the front of his uniform. My thighs trembled. I'd been scared shitless from the minute I saw the rat but I was only feeling the fear now. I was also pissed off with myself. A hundred grams of tobacco and ten phone cards wasn't worth this amount of shit. Nothing was worth this amount of shit. I'd been greedy and this was where it'd got me.

The Night screw poked at the rat's corpse with the end of the brush handle. It shifted and fell back. It was dead all right.

'The good news is he's definitely toast,' said the Night screw. He looked at me directly. 'The bad news is, I'll have to report you for smashing your TV.'

'Oh for fuck's sake,' I said, 'you can't be serious. I didn't smash my TV. It was the only thing I had to kill the fucking rat.'

'Yeah, but rules is rules. You know I have to.'

'You're just obeying orders,' I said, 'I understand.'

'I'm going to ignore that,' he said. 'Right, let's get some plastic bags and you can clean up all this mess,' he said.

Hayes called me to the class office near lunchtime the following day. A dusty TV sat on his desk.

'I heard you smashed your in-cell TV last night,' he said. 'Model inmate like you, I'm shocked.'

He blew at the top of the set and a little puff of dust rose up.

'Incidentally, I do know what an agnostic is.'

I looked at him, puzzled. I didn't follow.

'Before you and Ricky swapped, I said you were an agnostic and didn't do ghosts.'

I remembered now.

'Aye,' I said.

'It was crap point, obviously. Ghosts have nothing to do with God. I was just slabbering, saying the first words that came into my head, putting on a show for our friend Ricky.'

I nodded.

He went to the sink in the corner and returned with a damp J-cloth. He wiped the set and its wet surface shone.

'I think this was a surplus set that never went back to stores,' he said. 'It was in the cupboard. It's all yours. Try not to drop it on the way down to your cell.'

I carried my new TV away. Typical. First I was punished for my greed and then I was reprieved. I'd still have to pay off a tenner at the rate of fifty pence a week out of my earnings though for the broken set. I'd signed a contract to that effect and rats or ghosts or an act of God wouldn't change that. Not in a million years. But I wouldn't have to wait weeks while I paid the tenner off before I got a new set. No. I'd got one straight away. I could start watching shit immediately if I wanted.

That night I closed the toilet lid and weighted it down with books. No more night-time visitors for me.

Magic

It was a bit after half-five, the start of evening association. Magic was at my cell door.

'Permission to enter?' he said.

'Absolutely.'

Magic was six foot four and the top of my cell door was five ten. He had to duck to get in.

'All right, Magic?' I asked.

'Oh, top of the world,' he said. 'I love being in jail.'

Magic settled on the bed and then he opened one of his enormous hands and showed me a beautifully rolled joint with its end neatly twisted.

I smiled and handed him my Zippo. 'Spark up,' I said. I got up and pulled my door over and opened the windows between the concrete bars. As long as we didn't start roaring and carrying on we could smoke our heads off and the Day screws wouldn't come near us. I sat down again on the bed.

Magic lit the end and handed me the joint. I took a pull and began to count. I exhaled when I got to ten, and puffed the smoke at the window where it was caught by the breeze and carried away. Only one hit but I felt immediately calm and cheerful and humorous.

'Lovely that,' I said as I passed it back.

After we finished the joint, Magic took a lump of hash from inside his cheek and skinned up again. This second joint was stronger than the first. When it was done we split a Mars bar and I made tea and Magic talked about his life. That was the dope of course. It had made him chatty tonight. I'd had bits and pieces of his story over the time I'd known him but this evening I got it all.

His proper name was James Johnson. He was called Magic in jail after Magic Johnson the American basketball player. He was an only child. His parents were good-living Christians. They didn't smoke or drink or take tea or coffee or dance. His Mum wouldn't pierce her ears or cut her hair or paint her nails. His Dad ran a garage on the coast outside Coleraine.

Magic didn't like school. He started bunking off at nine and smoking fags at ten and drinking cider at eleven and shoplifting at twelve and using dope at thirteen and screwing at fourteen. His girlfriend told him she wanted hair tongs when her fifteenth birthday was coming up. He went to Woolworth's and stole a set. He hid them under his hoodie and would have run out only the store detective grabbed him first. There was a fight. He bit the bloke's ear and took a chunk off. He got six months in a secure unit for juveniles.

This was the first of many sentences. He was sent to training school and then the YOC many times over the next few years for shoplifting and affray and drunk and disorderly and nicking cars and possession of drugs with intent to supply and all sorts of shit. He went to sea with the Merchant Navy when he was nineteen but he didn't like it. Couldn't handle the routine. He got out of the marines and washed up in the midlands of England where he got involved with local criminals. When he was twenty-one he was arrested near the Bull Ring in Birmingham at the wheel of a car with a boot full of heroin. He told the police and later the court that he'd borrowed the car from a friend of a friend and he didn't know what was in the boot. He got eight years and was sent to Durham. He got a job in the kitchens peeling spuds and it was here that he met Danish Paul. Magic and Danish became friends and they met up in Copenhagen after they both got out. Danish let Magic poke his wife or so Magic said and then, because Magic had been at sea, Danish asked him to sail six tons of hash from Morocco to an island off the north of Denmark for a quarter of a million in sterling. Magic said yes and after many adventures, he got his ship to the rendezvous where, to his surprise, he was met not by Danish Paul but by the Danish police. He got ten years and was sent to jail in Copenhagen. He tried to contact Danish Paul but got nowhere. So he began talking to other prisoners, making inquiries. Did anyone know Danish

Paul? Yes, a few did. He persisted with his inquiries, and eventually he discovered Danish Paul had a second ship with fourteen tons of hash that shadowed his ship and once he was nicked and the Danish police had gone away thinking they'd done well, the gear on the second ship was got ashore. He'd been sacrificed, he realised, and the discovery made him mad. As he served his sentence he imagined killing Danish Paul and the sexy wife who he now understood was part of the plot to reel him in but when he'd half his time served he was deported and so he never got the chance.

Back home Magic began to ferry narcotics, mostly heroin, around the British Isles. He could take seven ounces up his hole and he liked to boast he didn't know another man with the balls to take that much up the shitter. He was always drunk when he did his runs. The booze made it easier to shove the gear up his back passage and it made him brave. Unfortunately, he was so pissed on his last run that he'd fallen asleep on the plane to Belfast and he hadn't woken up after it landed at Aldergrove. The passengers filed off. The air hostess couldn't rouse him. The police were called. They got him up. Then they ran his name through the computer and his record showed up. He was taken to hospital and X-rayed. The heroin showed up. He was arrested. He got four years and now, on the night we were talking, he was coming up to the halfway mark. As long as he didn't fuck up and complied with his sentence plan and did the courses and engaged with his Sentence Manager and his Probation Officer then he'd be out on licence once he'd two years served.

'I get my first parole, weekend after next,' he said. 'I just heard.'

Paroles were given prior to release to enable a con to adjust to the world outside.

'Where are you going?' I asked. 'Hostel?'

He shook his head. 'I'm thirty-eight. I can't go on like I have, can I?'

'No,' I said.

'I'm going home to the parents,' he said. 'We've been in touch. We're reconciled.'

'You never mentioned any of this,' I said. It was true. He hadn't.

'Didn't want to speak out of turn,' he said.

I understood. Cons don't like talking things up in case by doing so they cause them not to come about, or worse, having talked something up they then have to admit what they'd hoped would happen won't be happening. Cons hate to lose face like that.

'Probation have been to see them,' he said, 'and it's all been sorted. This was only in the last week or two. I'll have my paroles with them and when I get out, I'm going back to them, to live, full-time. That's the deal. I'll work in the garage for my father, get my head together, and maybe get some qualifications, AA three evenings a week, and no drink.'

'What about?' I mimed smoking.

'Obviously, I'll have to have the odd spliff. I mean, if I don't have some way of relaxing, I'll go completely fucking mad, stuck at home with the parents, but that'll be my only wee vice. Henceforth, no more crime, no more hard drugs, no more booze. Magic Johnson's going clear. He's turning his life around.'

I didn't slip across to 'E' wing to see Magic during association the next evening in case he thought I was after more dope. He didn't come to see me either. I did go over the evening after and I was disgusted when I put my head round his door and saw Tiny and Red Ken sitting on Magic's bed. The visitors and Magic were drinking tea and there was a half-eaten Jamaica ginger cake on Magic's little table. That would've been Tiny's. He'd a sweet tooth.

'Chalky,' Red said sharply. 'Bit of privacy, if you don't mind.'

You really are as ugly as fuck, I thought.

'Sure,' I said.

'We won't be long,' said Tiny. 'Come back in half an hour and then you and Magic can get on with your knitting or whatever it is you girls do together.'

I went to my cell and I didn't go back. I hated Tiny and Red Ken so much I didn't even want to meet them coming out of Magic's cell. I did go to Magic's wing the next night but as I got close to Magic's cell I heard Tiny and Red Ken laughing inside so I didn't even bother showing my face at the door. I just turned on my heel and went away. I saw Magic over the weekend though and we'd a chat. I did his laundry the following Wednesday. I bagged it up when it was dry and brought it round to 'E' wing. I found him on the landing outside his cell. He was ironing his jeans.

'Your washing,' I said. 'I'll throw it on your bed.'

'Thanks,' he said. He didn't sound friendly or unfriendly. He sounded wary, which was weird.

I ducked into his cell and left the bag and came out again.

'When's your parole start?' I asked.

'Friday lunchtime,' he said. 'My dad's picking me up.'

'How long are you out for? Two days?'

'No, four,' he said. 'Back Tuesday lunchtime.'

'Excited?'

'Not really.' Then he smirked. 'I'm absolutely shitting myself.'

Magic didn't reappear the following Tuesday. I listened to the screws talking the next morning and I got the story. Magic had done a runner and hadn't come back to Loanend from his parole, which, they said, Hayes included, was just what you'd expect of an untrustworthy druggie. He should never have got parole. They were agreed on that point. They were delighted too at this turn of events. That's something I've noticed. The screws always love it when a guy fucks up completely. Well of course they do. It keeps up the supply of men needed to keep the jail going, doesn't it? And you have to have prisoners, otherwise what would screws do for a living?

I was leaning against the door to the laundry room on the circle the following Sunday morning rolling a fag and waiting for the washing machine's cycle to finish when I heard shouting coming up the back stairs.

A few moments later Tank and Big Ben came through the door and onto the circle dragging Magic along between them. Magic was screaming and roaring and he looked terrible. He was unshaven and bloated and his clothes were filthy. Tank and Big Ben turned right onto 'E' wing, pulling Magic with them. I slipped across the circle and peered after them.

Magic's cell was halfway down. They got him as far as his cell door. Here Tank propped Magic against the wall while Big Ben unlocked the cell. Then the two screws dragged him in together. There was a moment of quiet and then they came out. Big Ben locked the cell. I was back in the doorway of the laundry room looking casual with an unlit roll-up between my lips by the time Tank and Big Ben returned to the circle.

'Hello,' I called. 'I see Magic's come back to see us. Did he have a good parole?'

Tank and Big Ben scowled and then disappeared into the class office. A couple of hours later I asked Hayes what had happened and he gave me the official account. Magic had had to sign a contract issued by Probation to get his parole. This was SOP. And it had the standard clause about not drinking. But Magic had come back to Loanend not only late, which was bad enough, but paralytic. So he was now on twenty-four-hour lock-up, pending adjudication.

Magic slept for two days. Then I noticed Hayes outside Magic's cell with a plate of dinner and fumbling for the key on Tuesday at teatime. I saw my chance and slipped up behind him. Hayes unlocked the door and pulled it open.

'Your dinner,' said Hayes.

'How are you, Magic?' I asked, looking over Hayes's shoulder.

Magic had shaved and changed his clothes but his face was covered with nicks and cuts and he'd a terrible black eye I hadn't noticed when he'd been carted in.

'What happened?' I asked. 'The folks drive you to drink?'

Magic rolled his eyes and shook his huge head.

'It's a long story,' he said.

I'd never seen him look so bad.

'And a tragic one,' said Hayes. 'Right, that's enough chatting.'

Hayes closed the door and turned the key and walked off.

'I'll see you, Magic,' I called.

'I doubt it,' he said morosely from the other side of the steel cell door.

I tuned in to the screws' talk the next morning. The Governor had ruled at his adjudication that Magic was to have a fortnight's cellular confinement in his own cell on the landing rather than the Punishment Block with no tuck except tobacco and no association. Magic hadn't grumbled when the punishment was handed out but instead he had asked if he could be a Rule 23 prisoner. This would mean he'd only come out to use the showers or to get hot water from the circle when everybody else was locked. Otherwise he would be in his cell twenty-four/seven. The only prisoners who opted for Rule 23 were the sex offenders and other hate figures, which Magic wasn't. He must've annoyed somebody very powerful. I decided to make inquiries. You need to know these sorts of things in jail because your friend's enemy often ends up being your enemy too. And the place to start was obviously Magic.

When Hayes unlocked me on Saturday I was up and shaved and dressed and waiting at the door. My bed was made. My cell was tidy. I was ready.

'Jesus,' said Hayes. 'I usually have to dig you out of bed. What's up with you this morning?'

I left the cell. He locked it. I followed him up the landing towards the circle.

'Well, I'm just so happy in my work, you see,' I said, 'and I can't get enough of it.'

We got to the class office door. Hayes stopped.

'Ha ha, what do you want?' asked Hayes.

'I want to go and have a word with Magic.'

'Just a couple of minutes,' said Hayes. 'Then come and get the grub on. We're starving.'

I slipped along 'E' wing to Magic's cell and put my ear to the door. I tapped on the door.

'Magic,' I hissed. 'Magic.'

I lifted the flap and peered in. He was in bed. He lifted his head.

'Chalky?'

'Yes.'

'Hold on.' He got of bed. He wore shorts and T-shirt. He came to the door. He lowered himself down and looked through the Judas slit and I stared back through the heavy glass at him.

'Chalky?'

'Who else?' I said.

He looked better than the last time I'd seen him, which was over Hayes's shoulder.

'You're on the mend.'

He put his finger to his lips and he shook his head. There would be no talking.

'Hang on,' he said.

Magic went to his rickety table and began to write on a piece of paper. I waited. Then he came back to the Judas slit and held the paper in front of the glass where I could read it. He'd written the following in slanting print:

PROMISED TINY AND RED I'D MEET THEIR CONTACT OUTSIDE ON MY PAROLE, PICK UP £3000'S WORTH AND BRING IT IN WHEN I CAME BACK. BUT I FELL OFF WAGON, SOLD THEIR STUFF, AND WENT ON BENDER. NOW THEY WANT ME DEAD.

He'd drawn a wee hanged man dangling from a gallows at the bottom of the page.

'Oh fuck,' I said.

The next time I was alone with Hayes I put him straight.

'You'd better get Magic off-side,' I said. 'He's got some very big enemies. They're going to get him.'

Not long after this Magic was shipped out during the lunchtime lock-down and sent over to the hospital where he was told he would do the rest of his sentence in the hospital where he would work as an orderly.

It was a solution but what silver lining doesn't have its cloud? The next time I passed Red Ken he gave off to me.

'Your wee mate, Chalky,' he said, 'we're going to fuck him up.'

'What're you on about?' I asked. 'What wee mate?'

'Magic.'

'What about him?' I asked. 'He's gone, hardly worth thinking about.'

'You're priceless,' he said and went up the stairs.

Once Magic left I didn't think about him anymore. I'd liked him. I'd liked his company. I'd liked his dope. But he was in the hospital and I was on the wings. He'd do his whack and go home to his good-living mum and dad and more than likely our paths would never cross again. Ever. That's what I thought.

Occasionally, when lads on the wing went over to the hospital to see the doctor or the dentist they'd bump into

Magic. At the beginning their reports were positive. He was doing well over there. But then this changed. Suddenly, Magic wasn't doing so well. He'd gotten awful thin and he was a nervous wreck. Finally, someone came back with the news that he was shitting blood, vomiting blood, and in a right old state, and had been sent to outside hospital.

I got the next part of the story from Hayes. In the hospital they cut Magic open to see what was wrong. His internal organs were shredded. They took out some stomach and some colon and some bowel and they fitted him with a bag to shit in. He'd live but he'd be an invalid for the rest of his life.

'Oh,' I said.

Then Hayes said he was full of ground glass which had been put into Magic's food when he was over in the hospital and after I heard that I stopped listening because I had the feeling you get when you're high up and you look down and the ground seems to be luring you to jump and you feel sick.

I guessed Tiny and Red Ken were behind this and they thought they'd got away with it. Well, I'd show them they hadn't. The next time I passed them I said, 'Good work. Well done. You must really feel proud of yourselves.'

'What's he on about?' asked Tiny.

'Haven't a fucking clue,' said Red Ken. 'That cunt Chalky's always burbling on about nothing.'

'Irony,' I said, 'is when you say one thing but mean the opposite. Like you say, "Oh, that's really nice," but really you mean, "You know what? That's shit!" Like you two.'

'Watch your mouth, Chalky,' said Red Ken and he looked down his huge sharp nose at me.

The Evil Twins went on their way down 'E' wing and I went back to my cell. Well, I'd said my piece but it didn't do me any good. Speaking out couldn't alter the facts. It was really shitty what they'd done. Magic was weak. He was never going to be a reliable mule. He was always going to fail. And having failed, they punished him. What was it about those with power? They just couldn't stop fucking the weak over. And it wasn't just guys like the Twins who did this. The prison were no slouches either in this department. But that was the way the world worked. There was fuck all I could do about it. Fuck all. I just had to put my head down and slog on. And so I did but it was at least a week after the encounter on the stairs before I felt right again.

Christopher Jenkins

I was buffing the floor in the circle with the polisher when they first brought him onto the wing. This was early December. He'd flat feet and long lank hair and a goatee and buck teeth and a paunch and thick glasses. I clocked him for a kiddie-fiddler straight away. He had to be. You can tell, believe me. Kiddie-fiddlers look like kiddie-fiddlers. His name was Christopher Jenkins.

He was assigned a cell on 'F' wing, my wing, top end, near the class office, and he opted for permanent lock-up. Sensible. No aggro. Nobody saw him for weeks. I don't think he even got the Christmas dinner. The screws forgot to bring it to him. Not that anybody cared. He was a root. Why should he be fed? Then one day he was gone. They put him on another wing in another block with his own kind, the Vulnerable Prisoner's Wing. He'd only been here until a space came up over there.

Then the holidays ended. What a relief. Holidays just meant more time locked in our cells. Normal regime resumed in early January and on the first Thursday afternoon of the New Year I slipped into the downstairs

Recreation Hall. The place was full of prisoners waiting to be called to the workshops or Education or visits. I felt great. Whoopee. I couldn't wait to get out of the block and over to Education.

Education was called, the grille opened, and I went through to the circle with all the ones going there, got patted down, and then was brought by an Escort screw over to Education, a caged area with doors at the back. It was packed with cons waiting to be called to class, smoking, gossiping, exchanging news, doing what cons do, and that was where I saw him again standing by himself, clutching a file of paper and a couple of Biros and looking completely fucking clueless – Christopher Jenkins. So he was going to Education the same as I was. I hoped he wasn't going to be in my class. I don't like roots because of what they done. And I don't like them because of what they attract – clowns who want to batter them to make a reputation for themselves. That makes the powers that be go mental and then they bring the Riot screws and the peelers in and then everybody ends up having a really bad fucking time.

Even though I don't believe I said a silent prayer while I waited, 'Please God, not my creative writing class.' But did He listen? Did He fuck. Classes were called. The screws opened the doors. We all filed in. I followed him through the doors and up the stairs. I kept my distance from Christopher Jenkins because it wouldn't do to be seen walking beside a dirty root. Other cons would think we had something in common if they saw that. Or worse, that we were mates. We got to the first floor. I watched him go down the corridor and into my classroom. Oh fuck. I went in and there he was, sat in the corner again away from all the others.

'Hello, Chalky.' This was Beefy. Armed robber. Doing eight. I sat beside him. He wasn't in my block so I only saw him in class. 'Good Christmas?' he asked.

'It's jail.'

'And I thought it was just a bad dream,' he said.

The door opened. Twelve men in the class fell quiet as she came in. Wearing a skirt that swished. And perfume. And earrings that dangled. Our teacher. A woman. With a woman's voice and nice hands. And nail varnish. The thirteenth man was Christopher Jenkins and he didn't fall quiet because he had been silent all along. Nobody talks to a root.

'Good break?'

'Yes, Veronica,' twelve cons eagerly replied. The thirteenth again said nothing.

'And who are you?' she said to him in the corner who hadn't spoken.

Christopher Jenkins opened his mouth but the only noise that came out was his tongue slapping about inside against his cheeks. 'Ch . . . Chr . . . Chri . . .'

Christ. A root with a stammer in my favourite class, the one that gave me two hours weekly with the lovely Veronica.

'His name's Christopher Jenkins,' I said.

'Thank you, Chalky.'

'Root lover,' came the quiet words Veronica didn't hear. It was Alan, sat on my left. Block 2. Drug dealer. Doing six. Unpopular. His measures were always slightly under. Before Christmas, I'd heard, some lads in his block gave him a tanking in the yard because they never got quite what they paid for. It hadn't done him any good. He was still the same obnoxious cunt. What was it he said? Me – a root lover? Me. I now imagined what I would say to him – 'Alan, mate, I'm doing twelve fucking years. Assault Occasioning Actual Bodily Harm. On a peeler. I hit him in the face with a brick when he tried to arrest me. Any more lip out of you and you'll get the same' – and then I thought about what would happen if I spoke. There'd be a row and I'd end up battering the clown and knowing my luck I'd probably cop another twelve years for it. So I didn't say nothing. I just sat there, steaming.

Veronica read us a bit of Laurie Lee's *Cider with Rosie*. Then we all had to describe a childhood memory. Then we all read our pieces aloud except Christopher Jenkins. Veronica read his. It was about his Dad pinning a mouse down with a plastic tube and the mouse running up the inside and jumping into his face. His Dad damned near swallowed it and we all damned near died laughing. Except for Alan. He just scowled. Jealous boots.

Veronica gave us our homework at the end of the class – five hundred words on a parent. Class dismissed.

I was excused my orderly teatime servery duties on Thursday afternoons because I was in Education. Torvill filled in for me. So I went and collected my tea from the circle once I got back on the wing. It was nice not to be the one dishing the muck out for a change. Curry. Apple pie. Custard. I passed Christopher Jenkins' old cell as I headed back to mine and I couldn't help imagining looking in, seeing him sitting on his bed, him seeing me and nodding cautiously, me nodding back just as carefully and then me saying 'Brilliant story today,' and then him moving his tongue inside his mouth and then after a lot of trouble finally saying, 'Thank you,' and beaming as he spoke and then me thinking, I was probably the first person to have said a nice word to him since he'd arrived.

Yeah, that's what I thought. What the fuck was happening to me? What was I thinking? But I had and because I was interested in him now and had to know, over the following days, when I was in the screws' office cooking their breakfasts and that, by a combination of eavesdropping, sneaking a look at paperwork that was lying around and asking sly wee questions, I got Christopher Jenkins' story.

He was doing four years for downloading child pornography. Did it on the computer at work. Lost his job. Lost his fiancée too. Aye, I know. How did somebody with his looks get a girl? But he did. Or had. Apparently. Anyway, she was gone. Ditto family, friends, home. When he got out he'd have to start life from scratch somewhere no one knew him. And he'd be on the register for sex offenders. For life. I actually felt a wee bit sorry for him by the time I'd got all his story.

Then, a couple of classes after I found out his story, he asked if I'd lend him a roll of Sellotape, which he said was unavailable on his wing, and I said I would, and I brought a roll to the next class, and the class after he returned it with an Aero – our transactions were conducted in the toilet, nobody saw, technically this was trafficking, technically we could have been charged – and after that we were nodding acquaintances, though never in public you understand and certainly not in the class, but when we were in the library over in Education, where other cons wouldn't see, we'd exchange a few words, and of course I never told him that I knew his story, and I took care I was never too fucking familiar. I didn't want him getting ideas, like I was his friend. I had a reputation to maintain.

In the spring, Veronica entered everybody's stories written over the course of the year into a competition. It was summer when we heard back about them. I got a merit for my one about my mate Sol and ten quid.

Christopher Jenkins came first and won a hundred for a story called 'Help' about his father being shipwrecked. Alan had high hopes for his piece about an escaped lion on the Shankill Road but he got nothing, nothing at all.

He begged Veronica to phone the competition people and check there hadn't been a mistake. He banged on and on about it.

'All right,' Veronica finally said. 'I'll go and phone. I'll be five minutes. Don't do anything I wouldn't do.'

She walked out. The door closed behind.

'There's a dirty root in the room,' said Alan, 'and he's getting on my tits.'

The men on either side of Alan nodded.

'If he doesn't fuck off, right now, he's going to get it.'

Here was the deal. Christopher Jenkins either left or else he'd get it, because he'd refused to do what he'd been told – not here, it'd be done on the wing: boiling water mixed with sugar in a plastic half-pint mug chucked in his face, a beating, a slashing, a stomping, something like that, nasty for sure.

'I've mates, good mates,' continued Alan, 'and if the root doesn't fuck off now, trust me, I'll just snap my fingers and they'll do what has to be done.'

Now of course Christopher Jenkins' wing was mostly roots but, as he knew, as Alan knew, as everyone in Loanend knew, there were one or two fractious cons in the mix on the Vulnerable Prisoner's Wing who were there as an unsanctioned unofficial punishment. These cons didn't like being with the roots of course and if they did kick off, well, the screws benefited doubly: a dirty root got it and the screws could then punish the non-complaint prisoner and what Alan was implying was that one of these belligerents was a mate of his and would do the necessary if Alan didn't get his way.

'Chris, I'd do what he says,' said Reg. Despite his un-Provo name, Reg was a Provo who'd been brought back after a domestic when he threw his wife out the first-storey window of their house. 'I'd go.'

Reg was the only one who ever talked to Christopher Jenkins in the class, which he was only able to do because he was a Republican and now that Reg was telling him this, Christopher Jenkins knew he had to go. He gathered his papers and rushed from the room on his flat feet.

'That's better,' said Alan. 'I can breathe easier now.'

The door opened. Veronica came in.

'I just saw Christopher at the end of the landing talking to an officer,' she said. 'He said he wasn't feeling well. He wants to be taken back to his wing.'

'That's right,' said Alan. 'He's got cancer.' A few laughed. 'Root cancer.' The laughter was louder. Even Reg and Beefy smiled. 'It's fatal I hear. He won't be coming back.'

'Won't he?'

'No, and a good thing too,' said Alan.

'I think I'll be the judge of that,' Veronica said.

'We're twelve now, much better than thirteen.'

'I didn't know you were superstitious.'

'You do now,' he said.

Veronica asked me to stay when the class finished and as soon as everybody was out she closed the door. She was wearing a silky dress and her hair had a marvellous sheen and we were alone and the skin of her bare neck was white and freckled and lovely. How lovely to lay my cheek there, I thought. This should have been the moment of my year, possibly my sentence, being in this room with her, alone.

'Who pushed him out?'

'Who?'

'Christopher Jenkins.'

I said nothing. I just looked at her.

'You talk to him, not here, but in the library, I know you do. Don't deny it. I know everything. So it wasn't you. And I know it wasn't Reg because he's braver than you. He actually talks to Christopher in class. However, given his politics, I don't think Reg will tell me, so there's no point asking him. But you can talk to me, not a problem, so I'm asking you – who did it?'

'This is a prison,' I said.

'Yes, I am aware of that. Now, who did it? Who put him out? I want his name.'

'I can't tell you.'

'Yes you will.'

'You don't do things like that, not in prison.'

'It may be a jail but that doesn't mean you have to act like it's one.'

'Oh yes I do. You know I can't say.'

'No, I don't. Somebody put him out and that man is not staying in my class. You will tell me who it was. Was it Alan? It was him, wasn't it?'

'Tell you and get a beating? No way.'

The door opened.

'Chalky,' said the screw, 'Escort's waiting.'

'I expected better of you,' she said.

'It's jail,' I said. 'Don't expect better of anybody in jail. Expect worse.'

'Don't worry,' she said, 'in future I will.'

Because she was only a teacher Veronica couldn't put me on report for failing to obey an order so she got a screw to do it for her. I'd been asked a question and I'd refused to answer it, he said, which in the jail's eyes is a crime. I said nothing at the adjudication. The Governor gave me seven days in the Punishment Block. While I was on the boards, I heard that Christopher Jenkins got a bad beating and had to be sent to outside hospital. When I got back to 'F' wing I didn't go back to Veronica's class but I couldn't even if I'd wanted to. I was banned from Education by the Governor at my adjudication. He said that my attitude didn't warrant Education. So that was that. It had been nice while it lasted but now I was back on the wing on Thursday afternoons, cleaning and buffing and making up Welcome Packs, back where I belonged, back in Wonderland, back doing my time.

Acknowledgements

'The New Boy', 'Eskimo' and 'Smurf' were previously published as a single story in *Standpoint* under the title 'The Strike'. 'Chums', under the title 'The NGI Guide', was previously published by the National Gallery of Ireland as part of their 2014 centenary celebrations. 'Clusterfuck' was previously published in *Prospect Magazine* and *An Sionnach* under the title 'Toothache'. 'Sweet Gene' was previously published in the *Dublin Review*. 'Engine' was previously published in *The Irish Times*. 'SC', under the title 'TB', was previously published in *Fortnight Magazine*. 'The ABC Con' was originally published in *Make Believe*, the online journal of the Design & Crafts Council of Ireland in October 2015. 'Cell 13' was previously published in *Clifton 35, The Clifden Anthology 2012*. 'Magic' was previously published in *Prospect Magazine*, and 'Christopher Jenkins' was previously published in *The Irish Times* and *From the Republic of Conscience: Stories Inspired by the Universal Declaration of Human Rights*. I would thank the editors of these publications for permission to republish.

I'd also like to thank Gavin Weston, Molly McCloskey and Mary-Jane Holmes for reading the manuscript so carefully and giving their expert advice on the contents, and Jason Thompson for copyediting an early draft with his customary care and attendance to detail. All mistakes are my own.

Finally, I gratefully acknowledge the assistance of the Arts Council of Northern Ireland, whose financial support made it possible to produce this collection.